NO FAVORITE CHILD

JACK HARTMAN

Fulton Books, Inc.
Meadville, PA

Published by Fulton Books 2021

ISBN 978-1-63860-836-3 (paperback)
ISBN 978-1-63860-837-0 (digital)

Printed in the United States of America

AUTHOR'S NOTE

This is a work of fiction. Names, characters, entities, places, events and plot lines are the product of the author's imagination or are used fictitiously. Any similarity to actual persons, living or dead, entities, or events is entirely coincidental. Mangia Qui restaurant, and its wonderful menu items and staff, are used with permission.

For Julie and everything you are.

I love you today.

PROLOGUE

If Nature, for a favorite Child
In thee hath temper'd so her clay,
That every hour thy heart runs wild
Yet never once doth go astray,
Read o'er these lines…

—William Wordsworth, "Matthew"

August 22, 2008
Leeds, Pennsylvania, USA

The grapes hit the parking surface first. The heavier items from the bottom of the bag crushed through the egg crate, and the cans spread the separated grapes toward her car. Her shoulder broke her fall. From under her extended abdomen, her right arm shot out in spasms through the mash of yolks and grape pulp. It was over in less than a minute, before a crowd could gather.

"You okay, hon?" The heavy woman with the short-cropped hair running toward her was also in nursing scrubs. "You work in ICU, don't you? What's your name, hon?" The woman caught her breath and leaned forward more from the neck than from her considerable girth. "You look familiar. You sure you're okay?" She reached out to help. "You're really far along."

"I'm okay," the ICU nurse said from her knees, still reaching to gather the steak and the green beans. "I have this terrible cold, and I must have gotten light-headed." Her Spanish accent was only slightly noticeable on words with more than two syllables. "I need to get home and call my husband." She pulled the baguette into the bag.

7

"I know you now," said the other nurse. "You're married to that cardiologist. You helped my grampa last year with the cancer. Up in the ICU. You were so sweet."

"Thank you." She stood slowly and walked to her car. "I need to get home and call my husband. He knows what to do." She opened the car door and placed the groceries in the passenger seat. *He'll kill me if I don't*, she thought.

"Your face is so full. With the pregnancy, I didn't—"

The car pulled away. *I hope Juan is on call today.*

"Good luck with the baby, hon!" The Good Samaritan struggled bending over to pick up the egg crate. *Geez, I hope she's okay.*

When she arrived home, the very pregnant ICU nurse put away the groceries, changed out of her scrubs, sat in her designated chair in the family room, and called her husband. He was with a patient when his receptionist told him his wife was on the phone. He replied over the speakerphone that he would call his wife back when he could. He read his patient's EKG, excused himself to phone his wife, and made one other call before he drove home. When he arrived, he told his wife the pills would help her cold. He drove her to the hospital like he was early for his Sunday tee time. He put his wife in a wheelchair at the entrance to the ER and explained his wife's condition to the admissions clerk he had flirted with the day before.

The ER charge nurse ordered the prenatal record from the medical records department. The ER nurse in the room attached the blood pressure cuff and pulse oximeter and hung the IV to deliver magnesium sulfate and labetalol. The ER resident ordered the medications and inserted a central venous pressure line. The ER desk clerk paged the ob-gyn resident to manage the eclampsia. The ER nurse fastened the ID bracelet: *Lisa Sommer*. As soon as the ob-gyn resident arrived and evaluated her, they wheeled Lisa through the automatic double doors on her way to the ob-gyn floor.

Lisa turned to her husband, Dr. Derek Sommer, when she recognized the young ob-gyn resident by the side of the rolling gurney. Lisa again turned to Dr. Sommer when she recognized the chief of ob-gyn arrive in the unit. It was the last thing anyone could tell that she recognized. The massive seizure rocked her into the coma that held her life suspended just long enough for the surgical delivery of her baby boy. An hour later, Lisa was dead.

September 30, 2008
Zermatt, Valais, Switzerland

The sign on the glass door from the lounge area of the spa read, "Naked Zone." The four Americans entered in their white robes. Matt Morgan took the towel from his shoulder and hung his robe on the hook. Inside was a hot sauna, a temperate sauna, a steam room, a large area with several types of hot-and-cold massaging showers, and a massaging footbath. Linda, Matt's wife of thirty years, hung her robe next to his, revealing her slender body wrapped in her towel tucked tightly up against her underarms.

"You going in like that?" Matt asked.

"I'm here." Linda walked along the rock path toward the steaming footbath.

John Little hung his robe but kept his towel around his waist. He and Lindsey had been married for thirty-five years. John turned to Lindsey. "Sauna?"

Lindsey hung her robe on the other side of Matt's without responding and walked holding her towel to the hot sauna.

"What's up with Linda?" John asked Matt. "She went in with us two years ago in Amsterdam?"

"A lot of things were different two years ago."

Matt and John followed Lindsey into the sauna.

"I don't know," John said to Matt after he sat down. "I'm always afraid, with somebody as big as I am, everybody will expect me to be..." He looked down at the towel covering his lap. "You know, big."

Matt spread his towel and sat down. "You've worried about that since our high school locker room." Matt knew the clientele at this hotel was mostly German. "Trust me, John, nobody in here cares."

John surveyed the sauna. Lindsey was laid out on her towel, propped up against the wall in the corner of the top level, her near leg bent at the knee. Two young couples were talking in an unusual dialect, and the older couple across from Lindsey clearly didn't care what they looked like naked. "Wow, look at that pregnant fräulein. Beautiful, huh?" John cocked his head. "Sixteen weeks. She better not stay in here too long."

"You ought to know," Matt said.

"Hey…you hear about the woman who died with eclampsia last month up at Leeds? Wife of one of the docs. You know, I did my obstetrics residency up there, so I still hear all the crap."

"Actually, the hospital risk manager called me the day after it happened. Can you believe the woman was an ICU nurse?" Matt wiped the first drop of sweat from his forehead. "They always let me know as soon as there's an incident, so I don't develop any conflicts of interest."

"I smell a lawsuit," Lindsey said without opening her eyes.

"You going to get the case?" John asked. "No one's supposed to die from eclampsia anymore."

"I don't know." Matt lowered his voice. "It'll be two years until we see the lawsuit, and I really don't know whether I'm going to stay in practice that long."

"I don't see you giving up the law. Not at fifty-five."

Matt checked to see whether Lindsey was paying attention. "I'm not sure about anything right now. Linda and I aren't going to make it through the year. Hell, I'm not sure we're going to make it through this vacation. And I'm tired…of everything."

"I'm sorry to hear that, my friend, but I can't say I'm too surprised." The two men locked in on each other's eyes, but Matt wasn't really sure how much John knew. John turned away abruptly. "Hey, I know I've had enough of this heat." John took the towel from his waist and wiped his face. "I'm going to shower and go out in the lounge for another glass of wine. Hang in there, man."

Matt moved over to the level under Lindsey so their nudity would not be the obvious visual focus for what he had to say to her. He didn't know when he would get another opportunity.

"Linds, listen. Linda and I are getting a divorce when we get back."

Lindsey sat forward and looked down across her raised leg at Matt. Her thick black hair was flat with moisture.

"You need to work on staying with John." Matt averted his gaze. "I can't keep doing this to him. We can't keep seeing each other."

"What the—"

"Does he know—"

Lindsey crossed her arms over her breasts. "Why do you think I'm naked in here in front of John...in front of Linda, for Christ's sake?"

"Linds, you know how I've felt about you since—"

"Okay, I get it." Lindsey shifted off her towel and wrapped herself in it. "I'm not having this conversation in here." She walked to the door and turned back. "You disappoint me, Matt. You always have." Lindsey looked out through the small glass window of the thick wooden door of the sauna, in the direction of Linda. "You'll miss me."

Matt lay back into the same corner wall. When he exhaled, the perspiration angled in rivulets across his abdomen and disappeared into the deep crevices and hair below. The pregnant young woman watched Lindsey's exit and followed her out the door. Matt wondered what any of the sweating, naked Germans had understood. Matt closed his eyes. *Yes, I will. I will miss both of you.*

CHAPTER 1

September 9, 2010
Harrisburg, Pennsylvania, USA

"Hey, old man." Rick Dalton stepped forward to offer his hand to Matt. "What's this I hear about throwing some asshole plaintiff's attorney out of your office?"

"He's a bully, and I was done with him." For Matt, successful client development depended on appearing to like the people, the place, or the activity. Matt actually liked Rick, a veteran claims manager from the Pennsylvania Medical Excess Fund. Matt liked this bar, and Matt liked to drink. "And who are you calling old?" Matt took Rick's hand and looked toward the bar.

Rick had known Matt for over twenty years and understood the focus of Matt's gaze toward the Black woman who bore a striking resemblance to a youthful Diana Ross. At just under six feet and trim, Matt was still able to attract younger women.

"New lawyer at the Fund. She might be twenty-five." Rick gestured for Matt to look him in the eyes. "So finish your story."

"Bad case with significant injuries." Matt realized Rick was right about the look-alike beauty, and Matt had his own rule: He didn't date anyone younger than his daughter. "Jerk was taking my client's deposition testimony. He kept scoffing, smirking, shaking his head…all stuff that wouldn't show up on the record. So I put it all on the record. He called my client a liar on an issue he knew I could prove through the medical record and his own client's testimony. I told him I was embarrassed to have him as a member of the bar and ended the deposition."

"Well, from what I hear, that's not the best part," Rick said.

"He wouldn't leave and threatened to call a judge. I told him the deposition was over, so he no longer had any business in my office. If he wanted to call a judge, he would have to do it from somewhere else and get the hell out. He skulked out pretty quickly, and I watched him from the upstairs window walk all hangdog back up Front Street to his office."

"Crazy son of a bitch." Rick held his empty glass in the air. "Next round is on me."

"Dewars on the rocks with a twist," Matt said to the bartender and then turned to Rick. "Thanks, old man, but you didn't invite me here for a war story."

"Yeah, but I love the good ones. Listen, you know about all the changes to the Fund that are coming next year. We're putting on a dog-and-pony with the governor's staff for the Pennsylvania Medical Society on January 10." Their drinks arrived. "Could you sit on the panel and cover the expert witness changes?" Rick swirled his olive through the gin. "Your credibility with the docs might help."

"Sure." Matt rubbed his twist around the rim of the glass and dropped it in the scotch. "Get back to me with the details."

"So you started to see anybody else?"

"Why, Rick, after all these years, you hitting on me?"

"You really are a jackass." Rick sucked on his olive. "The governor's new Fund watchdog's a real looker." The olive was gone. "She's closer to your age, and I don't think she's gay."

"Great." Matt took another drink. "Sounds like the woman I would want to screw up another relationship with."

"I'll introduce you. You'll thank me, believe it." Rick downed his martini. "Hey, PAMIC put us on notice of that eclampsia death case against Leeds and the docs. Glad you're on board. I thought you were hanging it up."

The Pennsylvania Medical Insurance Cooperative provided the first $200,000 layer of malpractice coverage to all health-care providers in Pennsylvania, and then the Fund covered the next $1,000,000 layer as excess. A death case like the complaint captioned *Derek Sommer, MD, Individually and as Executor of the Estate of Lisa Sommer, Deceased, and as Parent and Natural Guardian of Louis Sommer, a*

Minor, Plaintiffs v. Leeds Medical Center, Marc O'Bannon, MD, and Juan Alvarez, MD, Defendants would trigger PAMIC to put the Fund on notice of the excess exposure immediately.

"Yeah, I pared down the office to me, my legal assistant, and a secretary. You know my personal life's a train wreck. My rebound relationship just ended, and I really was making plans to retire early and move to somewhere, anywhere else. Maybe to England with my daughter, or to Switzerland. The divorce has been hard on my daughter, so I don't know that's an option. The divorce was final last month, and I spent Labor Day weekend in London trying to work through all that." Matt finished his scotch. "But I don't know. When I got the call from Leeds that this case was actually filed and they needed me to defend it, and then they told me Jim Newman had it for the plaintiffs, I thought maybe I had another round in me." Matt looked Rick in the eyes. "Trying cases is about the only thing I do right."

"Newman's as good as it gets," Rick said. "You'll never be able to kick him out of your office."

"Don't want to." Matt raised his glass for the bartender's benefit. "That's the point of staying in the game. The medical records just came into the office before I left for the holiday weekend, so I'm not sure of the strength of our defense yet. Jim's complaint makes medical negligence sound pretty clear, but that's his job." Matt leaned in as though he had a secret. "One thing's for sure, with a cardiologist and an ICU nurse, there had to be something going on that's not in Jim's complaint."

"Something that ends with a woman going into preeclampsia and dying at a world-class tertiary-care medical center."

Matt took a long draw on his second scotch. "My bet is that there was some kind of do-it-yourself doctoring going on that ended very, very badly." He finished the scotch in one more swallow. "And it had nothing to do with my docs at Leeds."

"Money's always been on you, my friend." Rick pushed back from the table. "But you know we've paid out a couple million dollars on Alvarez on those other two cases last year."

"I always like a handicap, Rick." Matt stood to go. "I have another trial with Jim next month. I'll know whether we're going to do battle on this one by then. If young Dr. Alvarez dropped the ball again, it'll be your money that gets spent."

The two men shook hands. "You are a cynical bastard," Rick said.

"Working for you is what made me that way."

*****

The first thing Matt noticed when he finally looked at Lisa Sommer's ER records from Leeds Medical Center was the admitting history on August 22, 2008: "Patient passed out while shopping. (Seizure?)."

What the hell was she doing out shopping?

The next line was even more peculiar: "Patient went to her home and called her husband."

What the hell? Why didn't she go directly to the ER?

Matt was trying to understand this woman as he read the next line: "Patient waited at home for husband to return home to drive her to the hospital."

Matt realized Lisa ended up in the ER two days before she was scheduled to return to the prenatal clinic on August 24. He flipped back to the prenatal record to see if she had called in any vital signs. She was supposed to take her blood pressure four times a day, weigh herself daily, and test for protein values in her urine daily. She was supposed to report any blood pressure in excess of 140/90 and any increase in proteinuria. There were no entries after August 17. Whatever happened in the interim, Matt wasn't going to find out in the medical record.

He turned back to the ER record labeled Vital Signs. Lisa's admitting blood pressure was 165/112 at 11:43 a.m. Under Labs, her protein was 3+. Progress Notes showed they placed the central venous pressure line and consulted ob-gyn. Dr. Alvarez arrived within twelve minutes of the page. They ordered magnesium sulfate to prevent possible further seizures, and labetalol to reduce and control her blood pressure. Dr. Alvarez transferred her to the ob-gyn floor at 12:29 p.m. for further observation and a decision on delivery.

Looking at the ob-gyn chart, Matt saw no apparent explanation for the entry in Progress Notes at 1:55 p.m.: "Tonic-clonic seizure observed for 65 seconds. Patient's face and hands twitching, followed by arms and hands rigid. Patient ceased respiration for duration of sz. Limbs jerking mildly—relaxing, in tonic-clonic manner. Airway maintained, tongue blade placed, patient placed in left lateral position and secured. Mag. sulfate administered 2 g IV. Dr. O'Bannon aware."

It's time to meet with Alvarez and O'Bannon.

CHAPTER 2

Matt remembered the first two times he represented Dr. Juan Alvarez as a junior ob-gyn resident at Leeds and why Juan couldn't be trusted. He made a mistake. He lied about it. Twice. Juan no longer worked at Leeds and now practiced with an elderly partner in Hanover, Pennsylvania. Matt arrived at Juan's office and introduced himself at the front desk. Matt knew his physician clients never liked him to be waiting in the same room with their patients, wearing his lawyer's suit and carrying his trial bags. He was not surprised when the receptionist whisked him to the doctor's private office. Several diplomas hung from the walls, and files, loose papers, and medical journals were randomly strewn about the shelves and floor. Matt recognized the Leeds ob-gyn residency certificate, signed by Marc O'Bannon, MD, and he had seen the others when he met with Juan the first two times.

Matt reintroduced himself, and that appeared to create a moment of awkward tension in Juan when they shook hands. Juan seemed smaller than Matt remembered, and he was distracted by an unattractive shine on Juan's wavy black hair as he took his seat behind the small particleboard desk with oak veneer. The desk must have been placed to take advantage of the light that was angling in across the corner closest to the window. Matt pulled out the copy of the Leeds prenatal record and hospital chart, neatly organized, index-tabbed, and bound by his legal assistant, Andrea Barriga. Juan drew his hand across his olive-toned cheek and the wispy line of facial hair above his lip in apparent anticipation of Matt's first question.

Juan reviewed how he met Derek and Lisa Sommer at a welcome party for new residents two weeks after Juan had arrived at Leeds. Derek and Lisa were active in the socialization of new physicians of

Hispanic descent. Juan described how he seemed to connect to Lisa, whose maiden name was Hernandez, as a substitute for his big sister. Lisa gave him good advice about how to meet single women during his residency at Leeds.

"Derek was more distant and formal," Juan continued, "but he was open to interaction about medicine and sports. He would never enter into any discussions with Lisa about dating tips."

"How did Lisa come to be your patient?"

"She told me as soon as she knew she was pregnant. It seemed natural to me as an ob-gyn resident, and I guess it was natural for her to come to me for her prenatal care." Juan appeared to catch the implication in Matt's question. "We were friends, sure, but we were both medical professionals. Examining her was normal for me…and her. There was nothing inappropriate going on."

Too much information. Unnecessary. "Did your interaction with Derek change in any way once Lisa started her prenatal care with you?"

"Yeah, I guess. Maybe." Juan didn't seem to want to lie to Matt again. "Lisa actually told me that Derek wouldn't come to any of the prenatal visits. I couldn't believe he didn't come for the first doppler to hear the fetal heartbeat."

"Did Derek ever say why he didn't come?"

"No, but maybe he resented that we were close."

"Tell me about this entry at twenty-four weeks, after the July 4 weekend," Matt said.

"Derek and Lisa hosted a small holiday picnic at their house, same as always, for the three new Hispanic residents who started at Leeds on July 1. They invited me and six other senior residents of Hispanic descent. Lisa was relaxed and vibrant during the party. There was no hint of pregnancy-induced hypertension. She joked she was getting fat and happy. Derek overheard her, and when she went inside, Derek said to me—more like a physician than a hus-band—that Lisa was keeping up with her work schedule at the ICU and didn't seem to be tiring or having any unusual swelling or other signs of increasing blood pressure. I remember he said, 'I know Lisa best. She would go crazy if she just stayed home or had to rest all day. She loves her work, and the ICU couldn't get along without her.'"

"So the entry at twenty-four weeks?"

"Okay, see, I agreed with Derek, but I couldn't seem to reinforce that without offending him. He went off on me, saying something like, 'With my clinic schedule, I can't be expected to take care of anything around here. Lisa knew the deal when we decided to have a child. She's still responsible for the house and taking care of me here. And she'll stay responsible for the family after the baby is born. So she'll have to find a way to take care of everything here and still get to work.' Then, when I backed off, he laughed loudly, too loudly, and said in Lisa's direction, 'Just look at her. Doesn't she look great? Fat and happy, like she said.'"

"Sounds like we're getting to twenty-four weeks."

Juan leaned back in his chair. "I didn't know what to make of all this and didn't attach any medical significance to it at that time. I wanted to make a note of it at the twenty-fourth-week prenatal visit to confirm that there was no medical consequence reported by the patient, or her husband, from her continuing to work at the ICU. It made sense to me only later, on the seventeenth of August, at thirty weeks."

"Why was it significant then?"

"That was the first time Derek came to a prenatal visit, and he adamantly objected to the recommendation for Lisa to be admitted for closer observation, monitoring, and bed rest."

"I'm not getting the connection," Matt said.

"Once all the indications were clear, I told them that Lisa was in preeclampsia and that I was concerned. They both knew the criteria, and neither one was surprised. Looked to me like Lisa wanted to ask me for more information on what she could do, but Derek broke in and said she was doing well enough to keep active. She was just getting too fat. She would need to watch her weight, and by staying active, she would gain less. Lisa wouldn't say anything else in front of him, and I knew he wouldn't take me seriously alone. That was why I consulted Dr. O'Bannon.

"He came right over, and I talked to him and showed him the chart while Lisa and Derek waited in the exam room. When Dr.

O'Bannon and I went into the exam room, it was clear Lisa had been crying. Her affect was different, almost like she was afraid. Dr. O'Bannon made the same recommendation and expressed the same concerns. Lisa never said another word that day. Derek said they had talked about it and Lisa was scared by our comments. She wanted to keep working, and she was perfectly capable of monitoring her own blood pressure and protein values in her urine. And, in fact, she could do that even better at work in the hospital. I thought about pulling her aside and talking to her alone, but the situation was too tense. Lisa nodded when we set up the parameters for reporting her values, and both Dr. O'Bannon and I made a note in the chart."

Matt took a moment now that he caught up to Juan's meaning. "So what were you thinking after that?"

"I trusted her to speak up later or call back if she wanted to come in." Juan shifted in his seat, his head turned to the side and his left leg bouncing. "She was a strong, bright woman, and she knew the risks to her baby." His leg went still. He turned his head back to Matt. "I'm not sure she ever thought about the risks to herself."

"Why do you think she deferred so much to Derek?"

"Well, there's the cultural element. Derek is some kind of Boston blue blood, but Lisa's roots are in the Hispanic community. The hierarchy is pretty clear. Women are subservient to men, and any man in a position of power or authority is dominant. I don't know how their marriage was, though. Lisa never talked to me about things like that. Derek was always kind of distant, but I don't know. I just don't know."

"Did you see her or talk to her between the seventeenth and the twenty-second?"

"No. She didn't call in any values, and I didn't have any other contact with her."

"How about with Derek?"

"No, nothing at all."

Matt leaned in with both elbows on his knees. "What did Lisa say once you saw her on the twenty-second?"

Juan hesitated. "She went back over how she fell at the grocery store, and once she got up, she drove home to call Derek. She didn't remember anything about passing out or what happened leading up to that. She went home to put the groceries away and because Derek told her to call him if there was any problem."

Matt stayed forward. "Did anyone perform any test to determine whether Lisa really had a seizure at the grocery store?"

"No. Eclamptic seizures are self-limiting and usually last only half a minute. She could have had a seizure or gotten light-headed because she was exerting and her blood pressure was elevated. We treated it as an eclamptic seizure, though, because all the other criteria were met, and we put her on magnesium sulfate with a loading dose."

"Is there a set protocol for how much and how fast?"

"Yeah, and we nailed it." Juan didn't hesitate this time. It was the first time Matt noticed any hint of Spanish accent. "Labetalol, and hydralazine too. You know, to control the blood pressure."

"Why didn't you deliver her right away?" Matt sat back to take in the answer to the key question he expected Jim Newman to ask.

"She wasn't responding to the labetalol, so we switched to hydralazine. We couldn't get her blood pressure down, and we were concerned she might go back into seizure. Besides, her kid was strong. No sign of fetal distress. Ever. All our efforts were aimed at trying to stabilize Lisa first, then, after she went into her coma, to save her life."

"What drove the decision to do the C-section?"

"Didn't look good for Lisa. We figured nothing else was working to control her blood pressure or bring her out of the coma. We might as well risk the delivery to eliminate the root cause of everything."

That's one Jim will agree with. "Any problem during the C-section?"

"No. Dr. O'Bannon did it himself. No questions asked. The section didn't cause her any problem she didn't already have."

"So what did cause her a problem?" Matt stood and walked toward the window. "Why did her heart stop beating an hour later?"

"We don't know, and Derek refused an autopsy." Juan's lip was twitching, and he bit down on it. "We ruled out a couple of obvious things. Brain infarct, cerebral hemorrhage. Those would have thrown up signs with all the monitoring that was going on." He paused. "Does it matter?"

Matt turned his head slightly back toward Juan. "Only if it could have been prevented." Matt did not get emotional about the consequences of medical care. Sometimes it worked. Sometimes it didn't. Sometimes it made things worse.

"Once she was in eclampsia, her systems were a month or more into the disease process. If we couldn't control her blood pressure with the labetalol or the hydralazine or prevent the final seizure with the magnesium sulfate, then we weren't going to be able to prevent her heart from stopping in a coma."

Matt asked more questions about what Juan and Dr. O'Bannon and any other specialists or the nursing staff did. Juan did not identify anything that caused Matt concern. Matt made sure that there were no admissions against interest that could come out later. Of course, Juan told him about the departmental morbidity and mortality review, but that was privileged and protected from discovery. Matt already reviewed that report and was confident that it presented no clear bases for malpractice liability.

"What do you think the plaintiffs' expert will criticize?" Matt asked.

"Everyone will say we should have admitted her on the seventeenth, when she was in clear preeclampsia, but she wouldn't stay. Somebody might say we should have used intramuscular magnesium sulfate for the bolus, but the line was already in, and we didn't lose any time going IV. I guess Dr. O'Bannon's decision to switch to diazepam when it looked like she had magnesium toxicity could be questioned, but the baby was good, and the magnesium sulfate values were scary."

"Anything else?" Matt walked back to his chair.

"No. Not that I can think of."

Matt leaned in, hands clasped on the back of the chair. "How about that a mother died in childbirth in a tertiary-care medical center from a preventable disease process that was timely diagnosed?"

"Yeah" was all Juan said.

They covered a number of other things—another meeting for Matt to prepare Juan for his deposition, Matt keeping Juan informed of all new developments, Matt providing Juan with expert reports, Matt having the case reviewed by an expert after all the depositions were completed, and his obtaining a preliminary review from an ob-gyn friend.

Most medical malpractice attorneys had a stable of experts they could go back to who would be willing to testify at trial. They also had a select few physicians who would do a preliminary review to steer the investigation and identify the weaknesses but would not appear at trial. These specialists generally focused on their clinical practice and got involved on a limited basis because they trusted that their involvement would remain limited. John Little, MD, was one of these for Matt. Matt would get his review from John, and then Matt would have to find another expert to testify at trial.

When Matt left Juan's office, he drove back from Hanover northeast through Spring Grove on his way to meet with another physician in York on an unrelated case. Matt had never driven this way before, and he wasn't sure whether he felt nauseated from the sulfur fumes billowing out of the local paper plant or from the realization that he might really care why Lisa died. Then again, thinking about John made him think about Lindsey, and that always knotted his stomach.

CHAPTER 3

"What do you mean he's not at Leeds anymore?" Matt wheeled in his chair.

Sandy Nelson, Matt's secretary, just came into his office to tell Matt that Dr. Marc O'Bannon had unexpectedly resigned his position as head of the ob-gyn department at Leeds Medical Center.

"What did they say? Did it have anything to do with the Sommer case?"

"All they said at first was that he was going out west somewhere. Wyoming, I think. And he said he wasn't coming back." Sandy checked her notes. "He grew up out there."

"So we aren't meeting with him this week?"

"Not unless you want to fly to Wyoming." Sandy moved farther into Matt's office. "But they got ahold of him and called me back. He's returning to Leeds to wrap a few things up, but you have the trial in Chambersburg next week." Sandy sat in the guest chair across from Matt's desk. "That could take the week, so I scheduled you up there three weeks from today."

"Okay, nothing we can do about that now, but I'll need to explore that with the good doctor." Matt leaned back. "He's supposed to be a great doctor, and I need him to be a rock. Nothing squirrely. Not with Jim Newman on the other side."

"Speaking of the devil…"

"Yes, I'm ready for next week."

*****

Matt sat at counsel table in the large courtroom of the Franklin County Court of Common Pleas in Chambersburg. He enjoyed watching Jim

Newman at work, and now Jim was walking his expert through direct examination. The case involved a child who went into seizures following a high fever. The seizures were eventually controlled, but the child was subsequently diagnosed with developmental speech delay. Matt's expert was prepared to testify that the delayed speech was the direct result of undiagnosed autism, which predated the seizures and was not, in any way, related to the seizures, the care provided by Matt's pediatrician client, or any delay in providing that care.

Jim had his expert, Dr. Ho Chin, describe his cutting-edge PET scan technology to study the brain, identify areas of physical damage, and attribute a cause, such as ischemic injury. Matt's patience was almost gone when he heard Jim utter the welcoming, "Your witness."

Matt didn't want to seem anxious when he started through the preliminary questions and confirmed that Dr. Chin had reviewed the entire ER record. Once the ground was laid, the pace built up.

"Doctor, you expressed the opinion that this child suffered an ischemic injury to his brain from the seizure activity that occurred between 11:25 a.m. and 1:15 p.m., right, Doctor?"

"Yes."

"An *ischemic injury* means, in simple, layman's terms, lack of oxygen, right, Doctor?"

"Yes."

"Do you see the entries for the blood oxygen saturation levels from the pulse oximeter recordings?" Matt pointed to the blown-up copy of the ER record for the benefit of the jury. "Do you see that at 11:20, it was 96; at 11:45, it was 95; then at 12:05 p.m., do you see it was 94?" Matt took a step toward Dr. Chin. "You still with me?"

"Yes."

"Again, at 12:30, the saturation level was 97; at 12:50, it went back to 96; and finally, by 1:10, the blood oxygen level was still 94?"

"Yes."

"For the benefit of the jury, as they have already heard, the *pulse oximeter* is that thing that they clip on the tip of the patient's finger, and it continuously records the oxygen saturation level of the patient's blood, is that right?"

"Yes."

"From the oxygen saturation levels entered in this child's record during the period of the uncontrolled seizure activity, there is no evidence of low oxygen saturation that could lead to an ischemic injury, is there, Dr. Chin?"

"No. Not from that."

"All those pulse oximeter readings reflect normal or even high levels of oxygen saturation in the blood, don't they?"

"Well, those readings, yes."

"That's all the questions I have for this witness. Thank you, Dr. Chin. Have a safe trip back to Chicago."

Matt looked at the jury. He gave them what they wanted—a show. And now he let them see that he was pleased. Matt knew when to let the jury in and when to keep them at a distance. When he hit the home run, he wanted them to know it was time to cheer. This was classic cross-examination, asking only questions he knew the answer to and that the answer had to be yes. Matt was smug as he sat back at counsel table, and that was exactly what he wanted the jury to see. Matt had eliminated any effect of Dr. Chin's out-of-town-big-city opinion, and he could close to the jury with, "If the child never had a lack of oxygen, how could he have suffered an injury caused by lack of oxygen?"

Matt must have repeated the oxygen saturation values four times during his closing argument. Jim did all that he could, and he did it well. The judge gave the usual convoluted instructions on the law and sent the jury out to deliberate. When they returned less than an hour later, the judge asked the foreman to read the verdict form out loud.

"Was the defendant physician negligent?"

"Yes."

Matt's heart rate spiked, but he sat expressionless, exuding calm and confidence to the jury that just found his client's conduct fell below the requisite standard of care.

"Was the defendant physician's negligence a substantial factor in causing plaintiff's harm?"

"No."

Without the legal causal connection, the pediatrician was home free. Jim had proven that Matt's client ignored the page, did not respond timely to the ER to provide his pediatric expertise to manage the seizures, and did not order the correct dosage of medication when he did arrive. But the jury believed Matt's expert that none of that had anything to do with the developmental delay or caused any other damage to the child. Matt lowered his head in a show of tired gratitude to the jury. He was neither tired nor particularly grateful. Trial invigorated him, and this was the only correct result the jury should have come to. The jury's job was to mete out justice, and they had done their job on this day. It was Matt's job, and Jim's job, to try the case well from their client's perspective, and they had done their jobs as well.

"Congratulations, Matt." Jim offered his hand. "You boxed Chin in pretty well."

"Well, you beat up my expert too. Made him seem arrogant, and uncaring. It worried me because you were right. He thinks the medicine is the medicine, and he can't conceive how his medical conclusions could be contested in the effort to turn personal tragedy into money." Matt withdrew his hand. "He doesn't understand the game."

"You won this one. Nice job."

Matt had tried several cases against Jim and settled many more. Matt had won all the trials, but the settlements had netted Jim's clients millions of dollars over the years, and Jim 40 percent of that. "Next up is the Sommer case. Is that one you're going to be pushing hard?"

"Absolutely. Your guys killed a vibrant, young professional woman who was about to become a first-time mother." Jim started to put away his trial materials. "Eclampsia death in a tertiary-care medical center? Dr. Sommer is still devastated."

"So why did he want Lisa to come home and call him rather than go to the hospital?" Matt started to put his trial materials in his trial bag. "And why did they refuse admission when the preeclampsia was diagnosed?" The locks on the large briefcase made a loud snap. "A cardiologist and an ICU nurse? What's the backstory?"

"You think you can ask a few questions and claim checkmate?" Jim had a brown suede briefcase in each hand, balanced on either side of his $2,000 Italian blue pinstripe suit. When he pulled his chin up and to the right to stretch his neck, the bright-purple tie popped, then settled back in place inside the crisp white collar of the $200 soft lavender shirt. Matt appreciated Jim's style, and he knew what the clothes cost because he bought the same quality. "You of all people should be scared to go another round in the Alvarez corner." Jim took three steps and turned. "My advice, avoid embarrassment for Leeds—and yourself—and tender the PAMIC limits to the Excess Fund. I'll negotiate with their millions, and you can wash your hands of another dog."

He's talking about settlement too early, and he wants to get me and PAMIC out of the picture. Must be something he doesn't want to come out at trial. Maybe not checkmate, but check at least. "I'll see you at the depositions. I don't think you'll be seeing anybody's money anytime soon." Matt picked up his battered black vinyl bag, which seemed out of character with his wardrobe but was a gift from his mentor when Matt tried his first case. "Thanks, by the way. You did a great job, as always. Too bad we can't go for a drink sometime."

"That would probably get me kicked out of the Trial Lawyers and get you booted from the Defense Institute." Jim took two more steps and turned back again. "Your expert thinks we're just in it for the money. What about you, Matt? Do you ever think about them at night, the injured and the dead?"

Never. "Can't let that happen, Jim, any more than I can have that drink with you." The two walked out of the courtroom together. "Rules of the game."

They separated before the elevators. Jim held the doors open before he entered. "I'm due, you know, in court. In case you were thinking I didn't want to try Sommer."

He's really good.

"How's that cynical thing working for you…personally?" Jim continued. "You've always seemed like such a nice guy. Too nice to be that cold."

He's really, really good. "Not so well, Jim, but thanks for the personal encouragement." Matt's elevator opened. "To tell you the truth, I was about to walk away from all this. But then Leeds called me on Sommer, and I almost turned it down. Until they told me you had the case." Matt entered the elevator. "I don't intend to retire on a loss."

Matt cleared the lobby before Jim's elevator opened, and he hurried to his black Audi A5 Quattro. Settled into the burgundy leather interior, Matt placed his favorite CD in the center of the burled-walnut dash and put the car in cruise as soon as he was on 81. He was tired, and now that he didn't have to worry about the jury seeing it, he could relax into his exhaustion. All he could think about was getting home in time for tapas night at Mangia Qui. Grilled baby octopus, garlic shrimp, and seared tuna were certain choices, but he wasn't sure what else he would have. It wasn't a wine night, though, and by the time he hit the Front Street exit, he was ready for a caipirinha—or two.

*****

Matt ordered and finished his first drink when John and Lindsey came into Mangia Qui. Lindsey hit the room like an early spring. Matt sat erect and smiled as he stood, like his mother taught him to do for any lady. Lindsey was not just any lady. John followed, unnecessarily ducking slightly to be sure to clear the swirling ceiling fans. Some women turned to look at John. Some of them might have been patients, and Matt always wondered what that would be like, having exposed their most private parts to John's deep-set dark-brown eyes.

"Hey, Matt." Lindsey leaned forward at the waist and hugged him before he could complete his exit from behind the table. "What are you doing sitting back here in the corner all by yourself?" She turned her cheek for Matt to kiss.

"Great to see you, Linds." Embracing Lindsey now would have been far less awkward if it weren't for their affair two years ago. Matt turned to shake John's hand. "Dr. John." Matt lost his balance getting back into his seat. "What are you guys doing downtown?"

"Since you turned us onto this place, we come in sometimes when I'm off call," John said. "Can't get enough of Qui's duck."

"I'm glad you're here. I was going to call you anyway, John. Remember that preeclampsia death case from Leeds?"

"You took it?"

Lindsey sat down across from Matt, and his attention shifted to her face. "Okay if we join you?"

John helped Lindsey with her chair. "Like I said from the beginning, that shouldn't happen anymore."

"That's why I need your help." Matt looked directly into John's eyes and wondered, for the hundredth time, how he could not know Matt made love to Lindsey.

"Hey, hey, hey, boys. No business when I'm around, remember?" Lindsey picked at the olives as the waitress set two more places. "I heard you went to visit Dana," Lindsey said without looking up. "How's she doing over there?"

"Actually, it was a tough visit. Divorce just finalized and she's having trouble accepting that Linda and I aren't going to be Mom and Dad anymore."

"Well, life goes on, huh?" Lindsey pushed her chair back. "She's a big girl. We all get over things—eventually." Lindsey put her hand on John's shoulder as she stood. "Order me the risotto, hon, and a glass of the Gavi. I'm going to the ladies' room."

"Lindsey's right about Dana, but I know it's tough for you." John ordered the duck and a Chianti and placed Lindsey's order. Matt ordered another Brazilian special. "But yeah, I'll look at that case for you. Same deal, though, just a preliminary review to help you get started. No testimony."

Matt barely heard John's comment, and Matt truly did not understand, at any level, why he could not wait for Lindsey to come back to the table.

CHAPTER 4

When Matt woke up on the day of his meeting with Marc O'Bannon, he decided he had time to take the back way up to Leeds Medical Center. The medical towers loomed up out of the flatland west of Harrisburg and before the mountains. It really didn't matter that this tertiary-care regional referral and trauma center was not in an urban area because Leeds was a city in itself. Patients and their families, and the medical staff, could eat, get gasoline, fill prescriptions, buy eyeglasses, have a haircut, and land a helicopter. The original hospital was now surrounded by a children's hospital, a women's health center, outpatient clinics, and a separate family-friendly medical practice center. Hundreds of physicians and thousands of other employees came onto the Leeds campus every day, and most of them never had to leave for any purpose until they went home at the end of the day.

Matt walked along the familiar pale-green walls of the back hallway. He knew his way by the smells. Left at the end of the hall and he would pick up the aroma of steamed meat from the cafeteria. Right and he would catch the alcohol odor of the treatment areas. Straight through the double doors, and he would be in the morgue. The ob-gyn department was in the oldest section of the clinic. The hallway there was lined with a rich wood railing, with matching wainscot in the waiting area outside the cluster of offices.

Matt had no sooner given his name to the receptionist than the stocky man with the flat brown hair framing a large head offset by a squared-off jaw came through the interior door. "Attorney Morgan, I'm Marc O'Bannon." Marc extended his hand.

"Matt, please, Marc."

"Come on back." Marc talked as they walked. "Don't want you to worry about this resignation. I've been waiting for a chance to get back to my roots, and a small practice came up for sale. I don't expect to make much money or be too busy, but I'll be able to fish and hunt and hike as long as I'm physically able." Marc entered his own space and went behind his desk. "Sit down, Matt. I'm tired of medical administration and all this high-pressure practice here. Just tired of it. Nothing to do with Lisa Sommer's case. Sorry she's dead, but we didn't kill her."

"Well, then, I guess there's nothing left to discuss."

"Lisa had a blood pressure in excess of 140/90, she had gained more than two pounds per week, she had proteinuria, and she had edema of the face and extremities, blurred vision, and right upper quadrant abdominal pain. She might as well have come in holding a sign saying, 'Preeclampsia.'" Marc watched as Matt opened his trial bag and retrieved his indexed and highlighted copy of the medical records. "The worst thing was, she knew it. She knew she had all the signs and symptoms for days before she came in. I'm convinced. But she thought she was invincible, and Derek is a jackass."

"What were they trying to prove?"

"She was a well-respected nurse, and she could have monitored herself. But she wouldn't rest, and then Derek started all that 'fat and happy' crock of shit. Lisa might have been getting fat, but she sure as hell wasn't happy. She was not a stupid or a timid woman. I've watched her bark out orders to the residents in the ICU, and she knew, sure as shooting, that she had to go to bed rest. But once Derek spoke up, she didn't do a damn thing but nod. She was afraid of him. She was unhappy with him. And she was scared for her baby. I've been at this pretty near as long as you, and I've seen this behavior more times than you could possibly imagine." Marc's cheeks had turned a deeper crimson. "What I know for sure is, that beautiful human being passed out shopping for that miserable prick's dinner the day she came in here and died on my watch."

Matt accepted Marc's offer of a cup of coffee, and they started to go through the medical records. Marc didn't add much to what Juan had already explained. Marc agreed with Matt that immediate delivery would have been the treatment of choice for a woman in eclampsia, but since the fetus was not in distress, they tried to stabilize Lisa before the C-section. When Matt asked the ultimate question, he learned that Marc had actually paid attention when Matt gave his presentation to the medical staff on malpractice liability.

"How does this woman die during childbirth in a tertiary-care medical center from a disease that was timely diagnosed and was being treated?"

"The variable here was that we were not in control from the seventeenth to the twenty-second. That was up to her. If you don't get consent from a competent adult patient, you can't treat. That's a civil battery in Pennsylvania, right?"

"What could you have done between the seventeenth and the twenty-second that would have made a difference?"

"Saved Lisa's life." Marc slapped his hands against the edge of his desk. "If she had been here, we could have kept her pressure down and kept her from going into seizure. Derek might have had to make himself dinner once or twice, but Lisa would be alive to make him and their baby dinner for a long time."

Matt learned what he expected to from this meeting. Mostly he confirmed that Marc was a rock indeed. He would be able to stand up to Jim's cross-examination and convince the jury on the medicine. What impressed Matt most was Marc's ability to tell it like it is and lay responsibility for Lisa's death squarely on Lisa—and Derek.

The only way Matt would be able to flesh out his suspicions about the black hole from the seventeenth to the twenty-second was during the deposition of Derek, which wouldn't be scheduled for several more months. Matt would have to dig hard to be prepared for that deposition. He would start by drafting specific interrogatories and requests for the production of documents. He wasn't sure what he was looking for, but he was sure now that there was something to look for.

*****

Matt retraced his steps to the cafeteria and settled for pork and sauerkraut, a staple of his Pennsylvania Dutch heritage. He was in surprisingly good shape for the way he loved to eat, and the women in the lunch line looked at him in much the same way the female patrons looked at John at Mangia Qui. The two often picked up girls together at high school dances, not knowing which one they would be with once they got into Matt's car and drove to their favorite parking spot along the back roads of the Gettysburg battlefield.

Matt called his legal assistant and told her to put a package together for John's review and print out a standard set of discovery documents for Derek. Matt would add the specific questions when he returned. Andrea reminded him that Elizabeth Burns, the risk manager at Leeds, had scheduled all the nursing personnel from the ER, the labor floor, and the ICU who were involved in Lisa Sommer's care for meetings with Matt at half-hour intervals beginning at one.

Matt checked in with Beth at conference room D and then met with the ob-gyn nurses who were listed on the prenatal record first. They knew of Lisa as an ICU nurse, but none of them knew her personally. The ER nurses were next. Each nurse accounted for her entries in the chart and was aware of the signs and symptoms of severe preeclampsia. Only after Lisa was transferred to the ob-gyn unit did the nurses have a significant role in the management of her care.

The ICU nurses never saw Derek. Marc waited with Lisa the whole time she was there, and Juan was in and out. The intensivists managed her care, and they consulted cardiology, nephrology, and neurology. All these professionals had worked with Lisa regularly, and they weren't going to overlook anything. It seemed to Matt that everyone was resigned from the beginning to the possibility of her dying and they were making sure they tried everything not to lose her.

Matt tried to explore any personal interaction between Lisa and her ICU colleagues over the last weeks of her pregnancy that could shed any light on his investigation and defense. Betty Matthews did remember one time after the July 4 weekend that she told Lisa she should take it easy and maybe ask for some time off.

"She said that we girls couldn't get along without her there in the unit, and Derek—Dr. Sommer—couldn't get along without her at home." Betty revealed nothing with her body language. "I told her we could double up on things here, and I was sure she could get some help at home."

"Did you ever talk with her about those things again?"

"Once more. She had just been to the clinic, I think it was around the eighteenth of August. I remember because it was my husband's birthday and I was ready to get home that night. She was in a room, taking her blood pressure, and she ripped the cuff off and covered the readout when I came into the room." Betty paused, then continued with her first sign of emotion, "'Lisa,' I said, 'if it's high, go home. Or lie down here.' But for God's sake—I didn't say that to her—she needed to take care of herself."

"Did you ever find out what the BP was or whether she reported it to the clinic?"

"No, but we had a crapper of a day here, and she was running herself ragged." Betty went limp. "She never said anything, and I never did again, but when she turned around and saw me that day, she looked scared. And she sure wasn't scared of me."

"Why do you think Lisa refused to be admitted on the seventeenth?"

Betty stood up and walked toward the closed door. She stood straight and turned back toward Matt. "Attorney Morgan, if I knew I couldn't get out this door, I'd bang on it and bang on it till someone opened it up. It was like Lisa was in a situation she knew she couldn't get out of, and she sat there and hoped for someone to rescue her." Betty returned to the conference table. "But no one came in the door, and she didn't try to get help." Her tears hit the Formica tabletop before she sat back down. "All she had to do was ask, and everyone who knew her would have broken down the door to get her out. I wish I knew what I could have done differently, Attorney Morgan, to help her, but I don't know why she didn't try to help herself."

*****

Matt knew it was a good day and he took the interstate back to Harrisburg. He was anxious to answer Betty's question, and comfortable he could defend this case.

CHAPTER 5

"Wow, Jim's not only good, he's organized." Matt said loud enough for Sandy to hear him outside his office. When he returned with his lunch, he was surprised to learn that the package from Jim Newman, containing the answers to interrogatories, arrived only three weeks after they were served. Andrea knew Matt rarely learned anything of substance in discovery responses, and intercepted the package that morning to summarize the answers for Matt's review. Andrea also knew to give her summary to Sandy so she could put them on the proper pile on Matt's desk. He looked at the introductory demographic information as he opened his chicken corn soup.

> *Name: Derek Grant Sommer, MD*
> *Address: 1253 Avenue G, Brooklyn, NY*
> *Age: 37*
> *Children and Ages: Louis Hernandez Sommer, 2*
> *Spouse: Harriet E. Franklin, CRNA*
> *Date of Marriage: 2/17/2009*

Matt was stunned. He knew Derek left Leeds shortly after his wife died. His first wife. Lisa. The only wife Matt knew about. "What the hell?" *The son of a bitch got married again less than six months after Lisa died. How long could he have known this woman? Harriet? What the hell's going on in Brooklyn?* He skipped down the summary.

> *Employment: Attending staff physician, cardiology department, Brooklyn Memorial Hospital, Brooklyn, NY*

Spouse's Employment: Certified registered nurse anesthetist, anesthesia department, Brooklyn Memorial Hospital, Brooklyn, NY

"Here we go again," Matt murmured. *Who is this guy? How long had he known this Harriet? I've got to get Andrea on this with HR. And I've got to take Derek's deposition. And I've got to read the rest of this shit carefully.*

Matt pulled his soup toward him and moved his body up in the chair and the chair up under the desk to concentrate with all his being. Nothing else was significant until the end.

Insurance Collected: Medical, $37,546; Life, $2,000,000

"Holy shit!" Matt was now yelling. "That son of a bitch. That son of a bitch!" He picked up the phone. "Andrea, come up here, please."

"Do I need to bring anything?"

"Yeah, the police."

"What are you talking about?"

"Just come up. I need you to follow up on Sommer."

Matt reviewed the entire summary again before Andrea arrived. She was attractive and married, and Matt was as loyal and respectful to her as she was to him. Matt relied on her to find information on anyone from anywhere. "Check with human resources at Leeds and get Derek's entire file. Both files—the employee file and the credentials file maintained on the members of the medical staff. Also, get whatever you can on Harriet E. Franklin, CRNA license, in New York, and anywhere else, date of issue, where she went to school, when…and any prior employers."

"You don't want supplemental interrogatories?"

"No. I want an investigation, not discovery. I don't want Jim to know what we're doing." Matt paged through the summary, front to back. "Look into this home address in Brooklyn. Chain of title. How long have they been there? I've got a contact in New York if you need help from an attorney up there. I don't care about the expense, and Leeds won't either. But don't tell them anything yet." Matt pushed back in his chair. "Just do whatever you need to and keep me in the loop. I don't want to talk with anyone at Leeds until I know where this is going."

"Where do you think it's going? Do you think Dr. Sommer did something to his wife?"

"Yeah, I do. Yeah, for two million bucks, I do. And it sure didn't take long to get married to this Harriet woman." Matt picked up his calendar. "Are the doctors and nurses scheduled for deposition yet?"

"Yes, Dr. Alvarez is scheduled next month, and Dr. O'Bannon is the next day. I don't remember the date, but I'll call you with it. The nurses are set over three days about two weeks later."

"Get this stuff together as fast as you can, and book Derek's deposition as soon as possible after the nurses." Matt felt like he finally had a glimpse into the black hole that was the unexplained death of Lisa Sommer.

His soup was cold, but he finished it as he cleared his desk of the Sommer materials so he could concentrate on preparing for his depositions about a traumatic priapism the next day in York. He would call John at the end of the week and set up a meeting at Qui's to catch up and find out what he needed to know about the medicine. Matt now knew John loved Qui's sliced duck breast in fig sauce with polenta, with a glass of Chianti Classico, as long as he was off call. Matt picked up the medical records in the priapism case and started to read, "Patient hit in groin with four-by-four piece of lumber. In severe pain." *No shit.*

*****

"How did you get the night off from Lindsey?" Matt asked, wiping a drop of melted butter from the corner of his mouth. Mangia Qui was unusually crowded for a weeknight.

John finished his first glass of wine to quench the heat of the fresh chorizo with habanero sauce and was leaning back to stretch his esophagus. "You know she doesn't like us talking business around her."

"How were the artichokes?" the waitress asked.

"Great, as usual. And the good doctor loved the chorizo, as you can see." Matt watched her clear the empty plates from their back corner table. She never wore a bra under the black knit shirt of her uniform.

"I do see. Your meals will be right out, Matt."

"How are you doing, by the way?" John brought his eyes back from the waitress. "We don't see you very often since you and Linda split up."

"I'm staying pretty focused on work right now."

"Lindsey misses you, you know, and…well, things with us have been better ever since we got back from Switzerland. I'll have her call you to set something up." John laughed and asked Matt, "Did I tell you about the mountain weekend?"

"No. When were you up there?" Matt was glad to change the subject, but he couldn't believe that John didn't know why things changed in Zermatt.

"It's always the third week in October. Hell, I've been going up there for the oyster feed for twenty years."

As expected, John ordered the duck, and when the waitress finished placing their food, Matt was staring eyeball-to-eyeball at his whole striped bass.

"Another white sangria, Matt?"

"Yes, please. John, another Chianti?"

"No, I'm good, thanks." John watched her walk away and shook his head.

John had an uncanny ability to eat while he talked, and you couldn't even tell he was chewing his food. "These guys at camp are a piece of work."

Matt's sangria arrived, and he sipped at it.

"But you know, it's scary how much older everyone looks from year to year. This one guy comes in with an oxygen tank, all hooked up with tubes in his nose, and taking that break to breathe after every third or fourth word when he talks. I hadn't seen him all year, so I asked him what was going on, and he says, 'I smoked three or…four packs a day…you know…for years, but I…I was cuttin' back…when this here happened…and I got to take…responsibility for that…so bacterial infection…and the doc, he says…my lungs are fillin' up… with fluid and I…can't breathe and the…fluid stretches my lungs… so's the lower lobes…was hangin' into my ass cheeks.'"

They were both finished with their meals, and the waitress was back with the dessert menu. John shook his head again and leaned in toward Matt. "That's what your girl died from, you know."

"What?"

"You wanted to know what killed Lisa Sommer. The 'mechanism of death' was the question. Well, that's what killed her."

"The lower lobes of her lungs were hanging into her ass cheeks?"

"No, I don't think that's actually anatomically possible, but pulmonary edema, yeah, that was the mechanism of death. That's the classic definition. Fluid accumulation in the lungs with swelling."

"So," Matt asked, "did my docs do anything wrong?"

"Nothing they *did* do was wrong. The questions are with what they *didn't* do."

"Listen, before we get into this, do you want any dessert or coffee when she comes back?"

"I just want her to come back. But yeah, I'll have that chocolate Vesuvius thing and an espresso."

Matt ordered for John and added the usual lemon-and-almond Santiago torte and double espresso with a lemon twist for himself. "Okay." Matt put his legal pad on the table and pulled out the black Waterford pen that Linda had given him for law school graduation. He hadn't thought about that in a while. "Quit lusting over the waitress and lay it out for me."

"The problem is the seventeenth. She was already in preeclampsia and headed for severe preeclampsia for sure. She had a seizure at the grocery store on the twenty-second—no question—and she was in eclampsia by the time she got to the ER. You know this disease progresses from early in the pregnancy. In fact, there is literature that the recipe for preeclampsia is set when the egg is fertilized. So the only way the docs have a chance is to diagnose early, which your guys did, and manage and treat, which they couldn't do.

"We don't know what went on from the seventeenth to the twenty-second, except that the disease progressed unchecked for five critical days. Those five days made all the difference in the world to this girl, and in my opinion, she was dead on arrival on the twenty-second. No matter what you find out in discovery about those five days, it can only support my opinion because even if nothing happened, the five days alone without management and treatment took her over the edge. If you find out that she was spiking pressures or having earlier seizure activity, all the worse.

"And we're talking about an ICU nurse, for Christ's sake, who knew better. And a cardiologist. What the hell was he thinking? Once she was in the hospital, all the docs did what they could. Marc O'Bannon is a class guy. He was all over this thing, checking everything he could to tell whether she was going to respond. You can read a lot between the lines in the medical record. I think he knew she was gone, but he wanted to give her every chance to survive the C-section. And she did, and the baby was good. But then she crashed from everything that was already wrong back on the seventeenth. How much detail do you want tonight?"

Matt was catching up with his notes. "All you've got. I need to know where to go with this case."

"Okay. That's why I didn't have another glass of wine."

"Give me the grand rounds version."

"Generally, as the heart fails, it becomes weak and doesn't pump blood out as well to the lungs and other organs. A backflow occurs, and pressure in the arteries going through the lungs starts to rise. As that pressure increases, so does vascular permeability, and that pushes fluid into the air spaces, the *alveoli*.

"If the kidneys are failing, this buildup of fluid is even worse."

"Wait, was Leeds monitoring all this to know?"

"They were monitoring central venous pressure through a central line and knew, because it was high, the lungs were wet with volume overload. The kidneys weren't filtering, and the heart was failing. O'Bannon was looking at pH, and the values were showing acidosis. Metabolic acidosis resulted from the kidney failure, and respiratory acidosis resulted from the pulmonary edema. He could tell that from carbon dioxide and bicarbonate levels in the blood. She was already in a coma from all this, and there was no bringing her out."

"So what was Marc trying to do?"

"The only thing I could have thought of was where O'Bannon was going next when he decided to section her and get the baby out. You can tell from the labs what he was thinking, but he was a savvy guy and figured he didn't need the additional information at that point. He did the C-section before the fetus crashed, and Lisa Sommer ended up a bad statistic for Leeds."

"But what were you thinking Marc could have done?"

"Well, it doesn't treat anything, and O'Bannon didn't seem to need it, but he could have had a Swan-Ganz catheter put in to better monitor the treatment. Instead of a CVP line alone, you put the thing down through the right atrium into the right ventricle, on through the pulmonary artery, until the balloon on the end literally wedges in a small pulmonary blood vessel. This provides the *wedge*, or filling pressure of the left ventricle of the heart. Supposed to be more accurate to clinically manage a patient in preeclampsia with a Swan rather than just a CVP line. The Swan has a dual lumen that lets you monitor the wedge pressure and right atrium pressure at the same time."

Matt had John repeat that last part so he could get it right in his notes. "So what's the advantage?"

"You use only a CVP, and you can overload and lead to pulmonary edema and a whole cascade of hypoxic sequelae, including metabolic acidosis and respiratory acidosis. All that stuff is ultimately in the hands of the intensivists in the ICU, and O'Bannon made a good call, in my opinion, to do his thing, get the kid out, and get Lisa to the ICU for the Hail Mary."

"Is plaintiffs' expert going to be able to testify that it was below the standard of care not to put in the Swan-Ganz?"

"Don't you always say, 'When a doc asks me if they can sue for something, I always say yes. They can sue for anything. The real question is, can they win?' So sure, plaintiffs' expert will probably say O'Bannon should have had it put in, but they won't be right. Swans are still controversial. In the wrong hands, using the infor-

43

mation incorrectly can lead to more aggressive treatment, which can be detrimental, or even more harmful therapies, which can actually increase mortality.

"See, normally with a Swan, a high central venous pressure means there's too much fluid, and a low CVP means dehydration. But what an OB knows is that in preeclampsia CVP doesn't correlate with pulmonary-end arterial pressure. So with a patient in severe pre-eclampsia, or eclampsia, you might think the patient is dry, give fluid, and kill the patient through pulmonary edema. With this woman, they gave what they needed to, they knew what her pressures meant, and they responded to correct the pH with bicarbonate. O'Bannon wasn't surprised by anything, and putting in a Swan-Ganz wouldn't have helped him make the difficult decisions he had to make."

Matt understood all that pretty well because he had done some medical research before he called John, but he would have to spend some more time going over his notes with all the medical records in front of him. "Could you send me a report?"

"Sure."

"Will you come to court and testify?"

"Nope. You know the deal." John relaxed back into his chair.

"Do you know anyone who could do a good job with this one?"

"I'll send you a name and address with the draft report, as long as you don't use my name or give my report to anyone."

"Okay. Thanks, John. I wish I could get you to go to court, particularly on this one, but I understand. You don't think there was negligence, though?"

"No, not by your docs. But I'd push hard on Lisa Sommer herself and that idiot husband of hers. When they went home on the seventeenth, they might as well have been in some third world country where women die from preeclampsia every day. That shouldn't happen here in the US, and it didn't have to happen to Lisa Sommer."

CHAPTER 6

"You know I met with Dr. Little last week, and he'll get us a report soon." Matt's desk was piled high with documents for a leg amputation case he would start in Wilkes-Barre on Monday. "Bring me up-to-date on your investigation on Sommer."

"Do you need me to do anything else for Dr. Maloney's case?" Andrea had prepared everything that was on the desk and obstructing her view of Matt from the guest chair. "When do you want Dr. Anders to testify at the trial?"

"Let's go for the fourth trial day. Till we pick the jury, the plaintiff puts on their case, that should be about right, but keep him flexible." Matt sorted through the documents and pulled out the file marked "Defense Expert: Richard Anders, MD." "Bob Connor is going to want that jury to believe our client misdiagnosed deep vein thrombosis, something all their elderly relatives have had in one degree or another." Matt opened the folder and went to the highlighted section. "And we're going to have Dr. Anders convince them this woman lost her leg because of heparin-induced thrombocytopenia. No problem."

"I'm looking forward to the trip."

Andrea often went to trial with Matt. He was looking forward to the trip this time too, for Andrea's company. "So what did you find out about Derek?"

"I'll need your contact in New York to follow up on the chain of title. The courthouse doesn't seem to want to divulge much information to a Pennsylvania attorney's office over the phone, and the records are locked to outside internet access." Andrea opened a file on her lap. "But I drove out to Leeds to get Derek's employee and credentials files, and I summarized them. There's nothing relevant except that he went to medical school in New York and did his cardiology residency where he works now, Brooklyn Memorial Hospital." She put the summaries on the edge of Matt's desk that remained clear. "I went on the internet and found two articles Derek had published as the secondary author under his residency program director. They were pretty technical, but they had to do with molecular changes in blood cells as a result of hypoxic insults to the heart and other end organs." She put the copies she was reading from on top of the other summaries.

"Anything about Harriet Franklin?"

"Well, pretty boring. She went to school in New York, she's only licensed in New York, and the only place she's ever worked is Brooklyn Memorial. And before you ask, yes, she was working there during Derek's medical school and residency."

"Where was she living?"

"Okay, didn't expect that one." Andrea pulled out Harriet's license. "The current address is on her license, of course, but I'll have to check about before."

"Did I ever have you get phone records from the source?"

"No, we never did that before."

"I have, before your time. In fact, it was how I started my own firm."

"Sounds like a story."

"Yeah, but I'm embarrassed to tell you the details of the case. Sex, drugs, but no rock and roll. Point is, I pushed an investigation too hard for my client—even after they told me not too. Insurance company paid out way too much, and my senior partner told me to move on, it wasn't my money." Matt was lost in the memory. "I couldn't practice law that way. Safe. No creativity. I left that day and started my own firm."

"Maybe you can fill in the gory details on the way to Wilkes-Barre."

"I think I was right then, and I think I'm right this time. Prepare supplemental interrogatories and requests for production of documents for Derek to produce all his home phone bills from two years before Lisa's death until he moved from Leeds. Cell phone too. Then get Beth, up at Leeds, to pull the phone records for the cardiology department from two years before Lisa's death to until Derek left Leeds. If she gives you any problem, tell her we need to…check possible referral calls in preparation for the depositions."

"You still don't want Beth to know what you're doing?"

"No." Matt was on a roll. "Then prepare subpoenas for phone company records—land and cell—for Harriet Franklin, company name and address to be provided, and for the anesthesia department at Brooklyn Memorial Hospital, and for the phone companies providing service to those places—name or names to be provided. I want to be able to pull the trigger as soon as Derek's deposition is over."

"That's how we'll get the names and addresses we'll need?"

"I'll have them by then." Matt pulled a card from his old-style rolodex. "Here, this is the guy in New York. Try to get that chain of title, and maybe he'll know what phone companies serve the house and Brooklyn Memorial." Matt stood up. "I'll bet you a bowl of soup that Harriet Franklin has owned that house since they worked together at Brooklyn Memorial while Derek was in med school—or his residency, at least. What I want to find out is how much they were in touch, so to speak, before Lisa died."

Andrea got up to go. "I'll get started and see what I can find out before we go to Wilkes-Barre."

"And see if there are any marriage records for Harriet Franklin."

*****

The trip to Wilkes-Barre on Monday was uneventful. The section of 81 from Frackville to Hazelton is known for dense fog and slick spots in bad weather. Traveling in November was always risky, and the stress of the trial was enough without having to worry about the roads. The first day of the plaintiff's case went in as expected.

"It's not about the facts," Matt said to Andrea at defense counsel table in courtroom 4 of the Luzern County Courthouse. "This case didn't settle because Bob Conner believed in his facts and he had a plaintiff with an amputated leg. Could have been a big verdict."

"You don't think the jury is believing his case?"

"Not so far. Not on the facts, but Bob's expert was really good. Boring, but good on the medicine." Matt laid out his notes and the documents that Andrea had organized, indexed, and cross-referenced. "Defendant calls Dr. Richard Anders," Matt said to the judge, then turned to Andrea. "This is for all the marbles."

Bob's hematology researcher had taken two hours of explanation to the jury on how the plaintiff's blood clots resulted from deep vein thrombosis as a result of Dr. Maloney failing to recognize the problem and call for surgery sooner. Dr. Anders took less than thirty minutes to convince them that the blood clots were formed by a low platelet count caused by heparin-induced thrombocytopenia. He put the exhibits from plaintiff's expert up on one easel and then methodically drew on a blank sheet of paper on an adjacent easel how tapioca pearls stick together to form pudding. Matt wasn't sure how he was going to get the jury to understand his sophisticated, alternative explanation, but tapioca pudding never crossed his mind. Once Dr. Anders started down the path, Matt lofted his questions like softballs. He allowed his expert to transport the jury to the kitchen for a cooking lesson in tapioca pudding as an analogy to explain how this woman's blood clots formed from the unexpected effects of heparin actually causing the platelets to stick together rather than break apart.

Matt always learned something at trial, and always from Bob Conner. Bob was a consummate trial attorney whose only possible flaw was getting too passionate about his client's plight. Bob would get red in the face and all along the top of his shaved head. He sometimes seemed angry at the jury for even considering the theories thrown up by the defense to thwart justice for his injured and innocent client. That day, during Bob's closing argument, Matt learned a little Shakespearean history. Bob was at the end of a forty-minute tear and had just come to the HIT theory.

"Now, finally, ladies and gentlemen, this defense theory. This tapioca-pudding theory of heparin-induced thrombocytopenia. You heard my expert, Dr. Jessica Pritchard, explain away HIT, and I'll call it HIT from now on. HIT. Tapioca pudding. It doesn't get any sillier than that, so I'll just call it HIT. Actually, I'll call it a red herring because that's all it is. Do you know where that phrase came from, *red herring*? You know what it is, something you don't have to pay attention to because it isn't really important. But do you know the derivation of the term?

"Well, ladies and gentlemen of the jury, I'll tell you where it came from because that's all it is in this case. You see, back in the days of Shakespeare, when he put his plays on in front of a rowdy crowd without any formal stage, and no place to change costumes, and no way to change the sets, and men were playing women's roles, even in *Romeo and Juliet*, what they used to do was have a guy in a jester's outfit—you know what that is, a clown—come in front of the stage when they had to change costumes or change the set, and he would drag a dirty, smelly, oily, stinky red herring behind him through the crowd to distract their attention. They would be disgusted with the smell and turn away from the jester and this red herring, and they could get on with whatever they had to for the next scene.

"That's what this HIT theory is, this tapioca-pudding defense. A red herring. A dirty, smelly, stinky distraction from what is important in this case. And you know what is important. My client lost her leg." Bob finished out with the standard stuff of plaintiff's closing arguments.

Matt had no idea if the derivation was historically correct, but hearing Bob's version sounded great. Matt made a note to steal the "red herring" story. Bob had no choice. He knew the case would rise or fall on the HIT theory, and he had to embrace and defuse it head-on in his closing. It was a wonderfully creative effort from one of the plaintiff's attorneys Matt most admired in the courtroom.

The jury returned a defense verdict for all defendants. Bob was gracious, and all defense counsel and defendants wished the plaintiff well. Matt liked spending his days in court, and this trial had taken seven days. Matt left Andrea to pack up, and he went down the hall to the restroom. He passed Judge Camby coming the other way, returning to his chambers after excusing and thanking the jury for their service.

"It was your tapioca guy who convinced them, Matt. He was really good. Nice job. Good to see you again."

Tom Camby didn't miss a beat in his step as he talked to Matt on his way by. Tom had been a law clerk for Matt twenty-five years before, but now he was Judge Camby. They liked and respected each other, but the case was over, and there was nothing more to say. Matt and Andrea said their goodbyes to Dr. Maloney. No matter how close they became to a physician-client throughout their representation, once the case was over, the doctors never wanted to think about it again. Theirs was a perfunctory handshake, at best, as though both the doctor and his lawyer knew they had done their jobs properly and professionally.

Andrea rode up with Matt this time, so they drove back together to get her car at the office. They talked mostly about things at work and things in Andrea's life, but never about things in Matt's life. They were almost to Harrisburg before they talked about the Sommer case.

"Your New York lawyer friend had the title searched," Andrea started. "It's been in Harriet's name since before she and Derek worked together at Brooklyn Memorial. The title was passed to her from her parents."

"Had to be." Matt liked to be right.

"He also got me the names of the telephone service providers for the house and the hospital. The phone bills for the cardiology department at Leeds are in the mail. You told me to say what I needed to, so I had to tell Beth that you were concerned for the timing of the consult to cardiology and couldn't establish from the records or the witnesses whether the doctor who responded was at home or in the department when the page was received. I told her you needed the records for two years prior to compare the likelihood of where the on-call cardiologists most often received their pages on a statistical basis."

"And she bought that?"

"It was the best I could come up with, but she said she would send them."

"Great job." Matt pulled in the lot beside Andrea's red Mazda 4. "Good night. Thanks for everything. Always." Andrea stepped out. "See you tomorrow, unless you want to take some comp time." Matt always offered, but he knew she wouldn't take it. Andrea loved her work, thankfully, and apparently loved working with Matt. He always characterized it that way—working *with* him, not *for* him.

"Good night! You're welcome, Matt. Always." She smiled with the repetition of the sentiment.

This was one of the few times Matt had a true friendship and respect for an attractive woman without the attraction getting in the way. She was that good, and that nice, and he could never take advantage of her. He never wanted to. Andrea appeared to be equally secure, which was why they could comfortably travel all over Central Pennsylvania for out-of-town trials a week at a time. Matt actually thought about all this driving to his house after stopping for a sub.

Matt's answering machine was indicating a message when he walked into the living room. He pulled a Sam Smith Oatmeal Stout out of the refrigerator and a frosted mug from the freezer. He sat by the bay window with a bag of Utz potato chips and pushed the Play button. The original painting across from him with the naked woman in blue, arms outstretched above her, beckoned to him. He drew on the smooth, dark beer with a hint of sweetness.

"Hey, Matt. Call me back when you can. It's time to talk turkey." Lindsey's voice sounded genuinely happy.

Matt finished his beer before he returned the call.

"Hello, Littles."

"Hey, Linds. I've been in trial for a week. Sorry I missed your call."

"John's at the hospital. Breech birth or something." Lindsey's tone changed. "Are you mad at me?"

"No, of course not." Matt wasn't sure where this was headed. "I thought you were mad at me."

"For a while." Matt thought it sounded like Lindsey was taking a drink. "But John said to give you a call and try to set something up."

"Yeah, we had a good meeting about a case, and he said—"

"Listen, Matt, this doesn't have to be hard. John and I are doing okay again, and…well, it doesn't seem like you are happy." Matt could now hear ice cubes cracking together near the phone. "Sorry, just needed a drink. But don't worry, I only drink when I'm alone or with someone." She laughed. "Anyway, I called to invite you to Thanksgiving. It could be fun to get together like that. Our girls will be home. You can even bring someone, if you want."

"Thanks, but I'll be in London."

"With Dana?"

"Yeah. She called while I was in trial. Her in-laws will be there for some reason, and she's cooking her first holiday meal. She calls me and says, 'Hi, Daddy. Can you come over and help me cook Thanksgiving dinner?' and of course—"

"Of course, you said yes. You'd do anything for her. When do you leave?"

"Next Tuesday, and back the following Tuesday. Thanks for the invitation, really, and let's do something else soon. It could be fun."

"Enjoy Thanksgiving with Dana. Maybe you could join us for the Christmas party at the club."

"We'll talk when I get back. Say hi to the girls."

Matt pulled out his favorite recipe for squash pie while he was thinking about it and set it aside to put with his travel bag. He pulled out another beer and a fresh frosted mug and turned on the television. The more he tried to think about something else, the more he thought about Lindsey writhing in his bed.

CHAPTER 7

Matt reversed the order of his meetings with the doctors so he could have the benefit of anything he learned from Marc O'Bannon to help prepare Juan Alvarez. Matt wanted his clients so well prepared that they could answer correctly without appearing to play the game with the questioning attorney at depositions. No matter how smart and articulate the physician was, legal questioning was the realm of the trial attorney, and even a bad one was better at the game than any physician. Matt knew Jim Newman was the best there was at legal gamesmanship.

Matt first remarked on the view from Marc's office at Leeds. He then advised Marc that Jim would probably start with the doctor's education, training, and employment history, then move on to his understanding of the diagnosis and treatment of preeclampsia and eclampsia, then walk chronologically through his involvement in the care of Lisa Sommer. That way, Marc would be locked into what the standard of care was before the questions on what he actually did. Matt told Marc that Jim would close with the attacking questions based on his experts' review of the medicine. They went through it all one more time, front to back, and Matt included the care of Juan Alvarez, and the ER and ICU doctors, and all the nurses. The only new issue was the Swan-Ganz catheter that John had identified.

"Well, you didn't let me down, Matt. You're as good as they say." Marc nodded. "I wondered when we'd get around to talking about that."

"I admit I didn't think of it on my own, but I get some pretty good advice when I'm working on these cases. Why didn't you bring it up yourself?"

"Because it pissed me off that I didn't have one put in when I got there. You know, they had a central line in, and that's okay. I didn't need any information from a Swan to tell me what the pressures were or that we were getting fluid overload. We had worse problems than that from the get-go, and I thought I could get that kid out safe and give Lisa a chance if I just kept the regimen going. Tell you the truth, a Swan-Ganz wouldn't have made a damn bit of difference to me in any decision I made, but I knew every one of those decisions would have been better supported medically if I had the damn thing in there and the numbers in the chart. I'm an old dog, Matt, but I learn all the new tricks. I only use the ones that move the ball from *A* to *Z*."

"We don't have the expert reports from plaintiffs' counsel yet, but—"

"Oh, I know. They'll hammer us for that—"

"Jim will undoubtedly—"

"I know that too. I'll be ready for him, and I'm sorry we didn't talk about it before."

Matt shifted forward. "Listen, Marc. How are you going to answer those questions?"

"I'll tell him professionally and politely that it's controversial, that it's not always helpful, and then I'll—"

"No." Matt stood and turned to the window. "Don't do that. He'll eat you alive." Matt continued to look out over the vast parking lot surrounding the Leeds complex. "Can you say you had all the clinical information you needed without it to do what you did?"

"Sure, I can say that, and it's true. But how does that help?"

Matt turned back to the doctor. "Eliminate the issue. Look Jim right in the eyes and take the issue away from him." Matt sat back down. "Remember, a jury is eventually going to have to answer two questions: Were you negligent? And even if you were, was the negligence a substantial factor in bringing about the harm—Lisa's death? Stick to the story that she was dead on arrival. Turn the tables by focusing on the seventeenth to the twenty-second, and Derek's attitude about not admitting her. And her own decision not to be admitted, for that matter." Matt wasn't making anything up. He heard all this from Marc before.

They talked a while longer, and Marc asked how Juan was holding up.

"The first session went well, but I'll tell you after Monday. I'm meeting with him again like this to prep for his deposition."

"I know his history with you. He wasn't a star here, that's for sure, but I think he's clean on this one."

"I trust your judgment." Matt stood to go. "And it doesn't sound like he's lying to me this time."

*****

Matt had to delay his trip to London to keep his appointment with Juan. He resented losing the extra weekend with Dana. Matt was used to being alone but was not comfortable feeling lonely. He knew it was not a good idea to reach out to an old acquaintance out of loneliness, but he now had an empty weekend. He called a woman he had a drink with when he was trying to forget about Lindsey and move on from Linda. The first date hadn't gone particularly well, and Matt hoped that at least the food would be good at Qui's this time. The Tuscan rib eye was great, and the conversation was easy, but then Matt hit the wall that prevented him from being comfortable in any new relationship.

"Thanks for calling, Matt. I had a really nice time." Angella was an attractive professional woman, articulate, entertaining, and seemingly interested in seeing Matt again. She started to reach toward Matt's hand, but it settled on the gearshift. "Love your car. Not too many guys drive stick anymore."

"Thanks for joining me. It was good to see you again." Matt got out and went around to open the door for Angella. He was done talking about himself.

"Would you like to come in?"

Matt was married all his adult life. He had flirted with many affairs and actually had the one with Lindsey. He had the six-month relationship early in his separation from Linda because he was eager to love again. But he didn't know how to handle this moment. He wasn't prepared to commit to Angella in any way, and he didn't enjoy casual sex. He wanted to be in love, and it would probably be easy with Angella. But then he would have to justify it with Dana, and he would have to admit that everything was over with Lindsey. It was too much for tonight, he thought. *Maybe when I get back.*

Matt walked with Angella to her door and kissed her cheek. "I had a nice time too. But with a full day and the flight to London tomorrow night, I think I'll head home."

"Call me when you get back." Angella leaned forward and kissed him lightly on the lips. "Have a nice Thanksgiving."

Matt felt like a schoolboy when he said goodbye. He regretted walking away the whole ride home. His exhale extended when he entered his town house, and it was the only sound. The foyer light did not spill very far into the narrow front room. The original wide-plank pine floorboards glowed in rich reddish-gold hues. The taupe walls were set off by the cinnamon elephant paw Persian in the center of the room. Matt left the Brazilian cherry wood-slat blinds slanted up most of the time to allow some light but maintain privacy. That night, whatever streetlight glow found its way through them created soft, angled lines across the pebbled plaster of the ten-foot ceiling. Without any other light, there was only a subtle flow of shapes and shadows as Matt followed his gaze into the front room. He felt lonely again, and he went straight to bed.

*****

Juan Alvarez was ready for Matt when he arrived at the office in Hanover at eight o'clock Monday morning. After he finished with the preliminary instructions, Matt started back through the prenatal record. Juan seemed to feel responsible for not being able to get through to Lisa after she was clearly in trouble. Juan knew he couldn't have admitted her without her consent, and he wasn't prepared to take a hit for that. He said he felt guilty because he couldn't get Lisa to want to be admitted for herself.

"Eliminate the issue," Matt said. "Set aside whatever you're feeling personally and lay it all on Lisa herself and her husband. Don't make it appear that Derek had any more right to decide for her than the physicians, though, because legally he didn't. I know it's hard and you liked her, but she had only herself to blame for whatever happened between the seventeenth and the twenty-second. Now, what about when you came down to the ER?"

"To tell you the truth, I didn't have much to do with her care in the hospital. The ER guys believed she'd had a seizure already, so by the time I arrived in ten or fifteen minutes, or whatever—"

"It was twelve, from the record," Matt said. "Better to be exact if there's a record."

"Okay. In the first twelve minutes, then, they ordered the mag sulfate, bolus and drip, and the labetalol. They took a good history, did the right exam, ordered the right labs. I mean, she was big-as-a-house pregnant and clearly in severe preeclampsia, at least, so it was textbook. They consulted me to get rid of her to the OB unit and not because they needed my assistance. They just wanted the bed."

"And what about on the floor?" Matt decided to wait until he locked Juan in on everything else to hear what he had to say about the Swan-Ganz catheter.

"Well, half an hour later—or what was it, 1:55 p.m., in the record? Anyway, she seized. Textbook again, but no one was looking for it, and the nurses responded with the intubation blade and restraints. I confirmed an order for more magnesium sulfate, which they already had drawn, and we got her ventilated. Then I called Dr. O'Bannon, and believe me, he was there in a heartbeat. Well, I don't know how long it says, but once he got there, he took over. I think he talked to me only to keep from looking like he was talking to himself. He never said it, but I don't think he thought she was going to make it from the beginning. I never saw him look like that."

"Like what?"

"Scared."

"And you weren't making any decisions with him?"

"Nope."

"Any concerns with the decisions he was making?"

"Are you kidding? That guy's good! I learned more from him in the time I was there than I did from the rest of my whole residency."

Matt went through it all anyway. The clinical management considerations, the C-section delivery, the transfer to the ICU, the care there, and then her heart stopping. Juan was right—when it came down to it, he hadn't had much to do personally with the care and treatment of Lisa on August 22. Matt decided to ask him anyway, "Did you ever consider, or did you ever hear anyone else talk about it, having a Swan-Ganz catheter placed instead of the CVP line?"

"I sure didn't. And I didn't hear anything either. First of all, we wouldn't do it. We'd have to consult ICU or anesthesia, but no, I mean…no. I don't think I would ask for it today, I mean, personally. It wouldn't do any good. I'd transfer a patient first and then let the intensivists decide. You know?" Juan looked at Matt.

"Tell you what, Juan," Matt held Juan's gaze. "If you get that question from Attorney Newman, just say no."

Matt explained and left Juan's office quickly. He was packed, and he drove straight to BWI for the night flight to London Heathrow.

CHAPTER 8

Matt thought about his visit with Dana on the way up to Leeds. He helped her shop, he helped her cook, he entertained the in-laws, and he even enjoyed a walk through Hyde Park. But he never really talked with Dana. They never seemed to talk anymore. Not since he left Linda. Dana was still his little girl, and she still wanted her own mom and dad. Matt knew that wasn't going to happen. So did Linda. So did Dana.

Matt arrived at Leeds for the deposition of Juan Alvarez and set up in the conference room with the stenographer. Juan had gone for coffee when Jim Newman walked in wearing a fine Italian suit with hand stitching around the lapel. Jim's signature gold-knot cuff links pulled against his French cuffs as he extended his hand to Matt.

"I haven't been back here since 9/11, you know." Jim opened his briefcase and set out his files. "That day is my only regret as an attorney. Sitting here through those depositions while the staff came in here to watch the towers fall on the television. I kept asking if you wanted to stop the deposition, and you said, 'My doc's here, we're here, let's get this done.' When they came in for the second tower and we knew it wasn't an accident, I felt sick. Our world was changing, and we finished the deposition."

"Well…" Matt let go of Jim's hand. "Let's get this one started."

"Okay, Matt. I see you've still got that cynical thing working for you." Jim sat and gave his card to the stenographer. "Where's Alvarez?"

The early part of the deposition focused on Juan's background and went pretty much as expected. Jim knew about Juan's other malpractice suits, and he decided it was time to make young Dr. Alvarez uncomfortable.

"So I understand, Doctor, you did not apply for a staff position at Leeds, you were not offered a staff position at Leeds, and this position you took in…Hanover, was it? That was the only position you had available to you when you finished your residency in ob-gyn here at Leeds. Is that correct?"

"Yes."

"I'm sorry." Jim put his hand to his ear. "I couldn't hear your answer."

Juan raised his head. "Yes."

"Okay. Let's talk about the early warning signs and symptoms of preeclampsia as you knew them by the time you first saw Lisa Sommer as a patient at Leeds."

Jim walked Juan through preeclampsia, eclampsia, respiratory acidosis, metabolic acidosis, seizure prevention and control, departmental and hospital criteria for delivery by cesarean section, and making entries in the medical record. Jim started his questioning from the records at the first prenatal visit. Jim pushed on the full nature of Juan's relationship with Lisa, and Juan closed off his body language and averted from Jim's eyes during the responses. Matt was glad he was not under cross-examination that day about the full nature of his relationship with another man's wife. Matt felt himself closing off. He wasn't used to losing his concentration in a deposition.

"Excuse me, Mr. Newman. Could you repeat that last question?"

"Do you have an objection to the question, Mr. Morgan?"

"Well, I'm not sure. I want to hear it again, and then I'll let you know." Matt expected Jim to simply say, "Sure," and have the reporter read the question back to the witness.

Matt was sending a message to Juan that he was supposed to listen more carefully to the questions and answer only within the guidelines Matt laid out in the preparation session. Jim increased the intensity of his questions about the office visit on August 17. Jim pushed on how serious Lisa's condition was and tried to get Juan to acknowledge the danger of potential life-threatening consequences, both for her and the baby. Jim tried to get Juan to admit that he breached a duty to Lisa by letting her go home that day.

Matt let the questioning play out. It didn't matter what Juan said. The legal issue was clear, and Jim knew it as well as Matt. If a competent adult patient does not consent to treatment, the physicians and hospital cannot treat. Matt was more concerned when the questioning turned to Lisa's course in the hospital. The questioning was brutal, and Juan tired quickly. Juan knew the medicine, though, and he responded with confidence on the times and the numbers and the doses. Juan knew they were all accurately recorded in the chart, but Lisa was dead anyway. By the end of the deposition, Juan not only couldn't explain that he couldn't accept that.

CHAPTER 9

Matt could have driven home and back again in the morning, but it was more restful to have a drink and a good steak and not have to get up at the crack of dawn to come back for the deposition of Marc O'Bannon. And he had no one to account to at home. The first thing Matt did after checking in at the motel was to call Marc and bring him up-to-date on the events of the day.

"Nothing new," Matt said. "Just wanted to let you know how it went. I told you I would. See you in the morning."

Jim Newman stayed at the same motel that night and had dinner at the same time and place as Matt. They nodded in passing but did not sit together for a drink or dinner. They both knew the code. And they would both have only themselves for company that night. Matt wondered what that would be like for Jim.

Having only himself for company after three scotches usually led Matt to thoughts of Lindsey. Opening the door to his room, he remembered standing with Lindsey at the door to her house that semester break when they were both back from college. She was in a long-distance relationship with John for two years by then, but Matt had driven her home after a night out with friends before John got home.

"I'm just thinking, Matty. Why didn't we stay together as a couple?"

The question caught him off guard. For all of Matt's emotional affection for her and his physical attraction to her, he never really felt any passion from her back then. Even when they kissed. And when they stopped dating in their junior year and John stole her from him, there was no discussion, no disappointment expressed, no sadness or regret. They just stopped. And he asked himself that same question thousands of times. And he never forgave John.

"I don't know, Linds. I know I wanted it to work."

"I think we were always too much alike. In high school we wanted all the same things, you know, to be smart, to be a leader, to be popular, to succeed. Wasn't much energy for us to want each other."

"Yeah," Matt said. "I guess we didn't have that 'opposites attract' thing going on. What do you want now?"

"Oh, I don't know, Matty. We just have such fun together. And God knows you're cute as can be. But we never even kissed, did we?"

"I'm crushed you don't remember."

She kissed him on the cheek. "Now I remember." She blew another kiss into the night air as she opened the door. "Good night, Matty."

Matt stepped inside the motel room, fell into bed without turning on the light, and whispered, "Good night, Linds." He fell asleep thinking about the answer to the question that had haunted him for the past thirty-five years.

*****

"Good morning, Dr. O'Bannon. Am I pronouncing that correctly?" In response to Marc's nod, Jim continued with the deposition the next morning. "My name is James Newman, and I represent Dr. Derek Sommer, individually and as executor of the estate of Lisa Sommer, and as the parent and natural guardian of Louis Sommer, a minor, in this case in which you have been named as a defendant. You are here represented by counsel Attorney Morgan, and if you wish to consult with Mr. Morgan at any time, just let me know and we will take a break for you to do that. If you don't hear or understand my question, please let me know and I will repeat or rephrase it. If you answer the question, I will assume that you have heard and understood the question and that the answer you gave me was the answer you intended. Do you understand these instructions?"

Marc nodded again, and Jim advised him that his answers had to be verbal so that the court reporter could take them down. She wasn't allowed to interpret a nod or shake of the head. Marc verbalized his assent that he understood, and Matt knew he had prepared Marc well. The first substantive questions focused on the prenatal visit on August 17, when Juan Alvarez consulted Marc. About the third time Jim implied that Marc had the legal duty to admit Lisa Sommer, Marc decided to set him straight.

"Attorney Newman, you've obviously done your homework, so I know you know that this disease process starts at conception and proceeds insidiously without discernable symptoms for months before there is even a hint of high blood pressure, protein in the urine, or anything else you have on your question list there in front of you."

"My question called for a yes-or-no answer, Doctor, and then if you feel the need to, you may explain."

Marc's face was intense, and he leaned forward into the edge of the large walnut conference table. "No." Marc gave a single nod, with his eyebrows arched high. "Okay, now you listen to me for a minute, Attorney, while I explain my answer. There isn't a single doubt in my mind from talking to these people—and I mean Lisa and her husband, Derek Sommer—and from looking at the chart that day, that they knew what I just told you as well as you do today and I did then. They made a decision. I didn't agree with it. Dr. Alvarez didn't agree with it. That was why he called me in.

"On that day, she didn't require treatment. There isn't any treatment at that stage. She required observation, monitoring, and rest. We offered that in the hospital, and she refused. We were done at that point. There isn't anything from ACOG, there isn't anything in any obstetrics textbook or journal, and there isn't anything in the law, which I am sure you understand better than I do, that says we can, let alone have to, do anything after she says no.

"If you have more questions about what I did to try to save her and her baby after she and her husband got smart enough to come in here, I'll answer them. But the bottom line is, from her decision on the seventeenth, that disease process that started when that egg was fertilized and progressed for thirty weeks had the capacity to kill both her and the baby every second of every day, no matter what we did." Marc sat back in his chair, breathed deeply, and prepared to be questioned harder than he would have been.

"Have you finished explaining your answer, Dr. O'Bannon?"

"Yes."

"Okay, well, that's how we'll do it in the future, then. If you feel you have to explain an answer, I will wait patiently, without interrupting you, for you to explain as much as you need to. Now, as you suggested, let's move to the twenty-second." Jim Newman then walked Marc through the record for that day, challenging him on every clinical finding, reading, lab value, decision, and result, even past the delivery and into the ICU. Marc was clear and responsive, accepting the facts as they were, not buying into any implications from the facts that he didn't accept. He challenged any conclusion within the question that he didn't accept, as he had been instructed to do by Matt. There was no mention of a Swan-Ganz, much to Matt's surprise. Jim's final question was "Doctor, wasn't the answer to the progression of this disease process simply to deliver her, and we will never know, since that didn't happen for nine hours, what would have occurred if she were delivered earlier, will we, Doctor?"

"Attorney Newman, I've answered that question several times before. The answer is yes. The answer was yes for the entire thirty weeks since conception. That wasn't a question anyone was struggling with on the twenty-second. We knew the answer to that one. The real issue was whether there was any increased risk of harm to the fetus by waiting if there was any corresponding benefit to the mother by waiting. The fetus was fine. Strong, thriving, with no sign…absolutely zero indication of distress the entire time. So what was the perceived benefit to the mother in waiting? We couldn't reverse the disease. It was poised to kill her. All we could do was try to stabilize her long enough to have her be in the best possible position to deliver the baby without the delivery, in and of itself, causing her death, and it didn't. She died because she was going to die from all the effects of eclampsia, which, yes, I knew at that time. I didn't miss anything, Attorney, or fail to consider or treat anything. I knew she was going to die unless her body, which produced this inevitable circumstance, could stop it…somehow. But she didn't. And there wasn't a single standard of care that I failed to meet in the process."

Marc was the witness Matt wished every client would be. Jim could have used his best tactical skills to try to get Marc to make a mistake or become tired and uncomfortable, but it was clear that Marc's stand on the medicine and the cause of this tragic result wasn't going to change. Jim would have another crack at Marc at trial, but for that day there was no point in the exercise.

Jim would now submit the transcripts of both doctor's depositions to his reviewing experts and undoubtedly ask them to call him first to discuss their findings. If he liked their opinions, he would have them prepare a report for submission to Matt and use at trial. If Jim was not happy with the opinion, he would simply find another expert who would give him what he wanted. That was how it was done in this game played by these two veteran foes.

Matt would do the same. He would submit the transcripts to experts John identified and Marc identified and ask for a verbal opinion first. Matt would have to wait for Derek Sommer's deposition to know if he could substantiate his own opinion. Whatever the experts would say, Matt knew that day that Marc laid the groundwork to bury that son of a bitch Derek.

Matt felt strong driving home. He would join John and Lindsey for the Christmas party at their country club, get through the holidays alone, give his presentation for Rick at the Fund, and then retreat to Mexico for a much-needed break.

CHAPTER 10

M att worked his way to the solid walnut bar in the back corner of the large ballroom, noticing the effort the country club
staff put into the Christmas decorations.

"How's my world traveler?" Lindsey quickly rubbed up and
down Matt's back as she circled in front of him.

"Pretty good, Linds. Merry Christmas." Matt relaxed the arch
of his back and saluted her with his glass.

"Are you seeing someone?"

"I *have seen* someone." Matt looked around the room and spot-
ted John on the far side talking, his back turned to his wife.

"Anyone I know?"

"It wasn't even anyone *I* knew." Matt took a drink.

"Aren't you an enigma tonight?"

"I wish it were only tonight." Matt swallowed more Dewars, but
it didn't help.

Lindsey looked up over her glass and swirled the contents
around, head tilted down and huge pleading eyes piercing Matt's.
"Dance with me later?"

"I don't know, Linds. Last time we danced didn't work out so
well, remember?" Matt did. It was their last dance at the prom before
John took her away from him.

"You keep going down memory lane, Matt. Okay, well, here's
my favorite memory. Just after the weather broke—earlier that
year—I just got my new show horse, remember? I came riding by
your house and you were out in the yard, hitting golf balls or something, and I was so excited to see you. I rode up into the front yard
and told you to ride her around the house. You were nervous because
of the English tack, but you got up and took off across the front of

the house and around back. I walked to the back to motion for you to keep going, but when she saw me, she stopped dead. You slid forward down over her neck and flat on the ground on your face right in front of me."

Lindsey laughed lightly and set her drink on the high top. "I laughed and laughed because it was funny at that time…it really was…but I knew how you felt." She got serious again. "I told you to get back up on the horse, you know, like they always say, but I knew you were humiliated. Teenagers and all."

Lindsey was squared off in his face now. "But then we sat and talked. We talked for an hour there on the grass, and you asked me to go to that prom with you. I was so happy then. It was like you fought through whatever you were feeling, and it made me so happy. Like you were fighting for me."

Matt lowered his head but didn't say anything. Lindsey shifted to catch his eyes again. Over her shoulder Matt noticed John was turning from his conversation. He was coming straight for Matt.

"I want you to fight for me. That's all I ever wanted."

Matt pivoted to John. "I was just coming to get you. Your wife's in the mood to boogie! I hope you brought your dancing shoes." Matt patted John's shoulder as he walked away from the bar area. He hesitated, then turned slightly back over his shoulder. "Hey, I have a Christmas proposition for you."

Matt turned back fully, facing John and Lindsey. "Listen, I need to get away for a week, and I don't want to go alone. I haven't met anyone yet, and you guys have that empty-nest thing going on now, so come with me to Cancún. Have you ever been there?"

"Wow, Matt, how exciting! No, we stopped at Cozumel on a cruise one time, but never Cancún. When do you want to go? John will have to work out his schedule." Lindsey looked at John pleadingly.

"Well, I have this speaking commitment next month on the tenth, but I have a place reserved right after that. Actually, it's not in Cancún. That's great, but this is a different kind of vacation. This place is about an hour south, in Akumal. It's close to the Mayan ruins and has lots of great snorkeling. If you'll come, I'll take care of the flights and the villa."

Lindsey picked up her drink and raised it in a toast to the idea. John raised his empty glass and asked, "You're not taking anybody?"

"No. That's why I'd like some company."

"I'll have to get a new bikini. Do I need both pieces?"

"No, actually you don't. Not at the villa."

"Book it," John said. "We're in."

"Merry Christmas, guys, and enjoy the dancing! I'm going to call it a night." Matt kissed Lindsey on the cheek and shook John's hand a little harder than usual. He wasn't sure what just happened, and he certainly wasn't sure what he just got himself into.

CHAPTER 11

M att saw Rick Dalton across the hotel lobby and went immediately to check in for the conference. Matt was prepared to discuss the stricter requirements for an expert witness to testify in medical malpractice cases. The governor's office wanted to spin these changes as a response to the efforts of the medical society for broader tort reform, and this presentation was designed to placate the activists in the society. Matt saw these steps as something like trying to put a bandage across the gushing hemorrhage of a severed abdominal aorta that was the phenomenon of ever-increasing malpractice jury verdicts.

Rick met Matt at the registration table. "Evening, old man. Thanks again for doing this right after the holidays. Let me make it worth it." Rick walked him to the center of the room.

"Brenda, excuse me." She was talking in a group with the governor's chief of staff, the general counsel, and the director of the Fund. "This is Matt Morgan. He will be on the panel, talking about the expert section."

"Gentlemen. Brenda." He took her hand. "Matt Morgan. I've heard a lot about you." Matt was a little uncomfortable using her first name, even though he was considerably older than she was, but Rick didn't mention her last name and Matt had no clue who she was.

"Attorney Morgan. Nice to meet you. I'll introduce you all, and then we'll follow the agenda until the end, when we'll turn it over for questions. I'm sure you can all interact to steer the answers."

The strength and length of her body matched her all-business personality, Matt thought.

After the welcome, the panel presentation, and several extremely hostile and untrusting questions by the physicians, an open bar was set up and finger food was circulated on large platters by servers in starched uniforms. This was familiar territory for Matt, and he relaxed into the free-flowing scotch. It was two drinks and half an hour later that he found himself next in line after Brenda, and he offered to buy her a free drink. He paid attention when she ordered a scotch.

Brenda Warren, it turned out, was the lawyer Rick told him about. She was the new chief executive assistant counsel to the governor. "Yes, I will be overseeing the transition of the Fund under these statutory and regulatory changes and the process of assigning counsel to represent the Fund." Toasting Matt with her drink, Brenda continued, "I am well aware you are the star of the stable of the Fund's current counsel."

Matt saw the opening in her austere, professional demeanor and responded to her more as an attractive and interesting woman than as someone who could control his fate with the Fund. "Let's move away from the bar to where we can talk."

After some introductory information about her background, Brenda opened up. "Yes, I come from a family of attorneys out of Boston originally. We all stayed where we went to law school. I went to Penn, my older brother went to Fordham, and he's the executive assistant district attorney in Brooklyn, and my younger brother went to Georgetown and works at justice in the district."

"Well, I'm happy to get together with you to provide my thirty-five years of insight or assist in any way." Matt sipped his scotch. "Where will your office be, anyway?"

"I work out of the Capitol building, and all my time will be devoted to this project for as long as it takes. I don't have a lot to interfere with my professional obligations right now."

"I'm not sure that's good or bad." Matt hoped he was reading her right. "But I'm pretty focused on my professional life now too."

"Yeah, this is about as relaxed as I've been for a while."

"And I had a head start on you." Matt leaned closer, smiling more, his gestures getting broader. He lifted his glass and reached for her, touching her along the back of her upper arm with an open hand, for no apparent reason. When she turned away from him, toward the window ledge, he thought he offended her, and he cursed his weakness for an open bar.

With her back to him, Brenda reached in her purse, took out her pen, and then turned and handed Matt her Office of the Governor business card, with a different number written on the back.

"I really have to mingle a little more. I'll take you up on that offer of your insight sometime. Call me when it suits you." She shouldered her purse. "Thanks again for being on the panel. And…" She turned in profile back toward the center of the room, clearly confirming her feminine lines. "Thanks for the free drink."

Matt put the card in his wallet. He watched her introduce herself around the room, and at a distance, he could tell more about her forty-ish body under the tailored business suit. Her short-cropped auburn hair bounced with her energetic head movements. He couldn't take his eyes off her. *She's a good-looking woman.*

"Was I right?" Rick looked at Brenda as he caught Matt on his way out. Matt barely acknowledged the intrusion. "How is the Sommer case coming along?"

"Yeah, thanks, Rick. I'm waiting for the experts to weigh in, but I'm going to be out of contact for a week." Matt kept moving toward the exit. "I'll call you when I get back from Mexico."

CHAPTER 12

Matt didn't have to wait long. In the week before his trip to Akumal, all three experts called. When Matt hung up from the first call, he thanked the esteemed physician from Philadelphia, honestly advising him that it was unlikely Matt could find a way for him to be useful at trial. Matt didn't realize the woman from Pittsburgh and the other man John identified from New York would prove equally useless. There were some technical differences in their approaches. Each focused on slightly different time frames and who might have had the first or last or best chance to make a difference. But the common theme was the same.

Without the insertion of a Swan-Ganz catheter, which all agreed was now the standard of care, none of the three could provide unequivocal support for the care of Lisa Sommer. Matt would have no leverage in his negotiations with Jim and no defense at trial based on these calls. Unless he could prove some intentional civil act equivalent to criminal homicide by Derek Sommer, Matt would need a strong expert report to make it past preliminary motions and through the pretrial phase with any competent judge.

On his last day in the office, Matt received a letter from Jim Newman. Jim demanded $3,500,000 for settlement of the case, which was only $100,000 less than the total malpractice insurance coverage available for all three defendants. That was no surprise, but it did surprise Matt that neither of Jim's enclosed expert reports mentioned the Swan-Ganz catheter issue. How could it be the central issue for all three of Matt's consultants and not mentioned by Jim's experts?

Both reports concluded that Lisa should have been identified as being at higher risk for preeclampsia, her early weight gain should have been a red flag to start more frequent monitoring, she should have been placed on medical leave from the ICU, her diet and activity should have been altered, and an available ACOG teaching packet on preeclampsia should have been distributed in the prenatal clinic. On the seventeenth, she should have been admitted, using the threat of damage to the fetus as the involuntary basis if the mother refused. The husband's input was ethically, legally, and medically irrelevant, and noting it in the chart showed it was given inappropriate credence.

Lisa should have been admitted immediately and directly to the OB unit on the twenty-second, the attending should have been called immediately, and magnesium sulfate and labetalol should have been given immediately, as they were, but only to stabilize Lisa initially for immediate C-section delivery. The common theory was that Lisa's eclampsia would have been eliminated along with the pregnancy that was causing it, the patient would not have seized and gone into a coma, progressing to pulmonary edema, heart and kidney failure, and acidosis, and she would have carried her healthy baby home from Leeds for a happy life ever after with Derek.

Now Matt understood. Under that theory, they never got to the point that a Swan-Ganz was necessary, or even useful.

Matt dutifully corresponded to the claims representative of PAMIC, the conglomerate that provided the primary $200,000 layer of coverage for Leeds and its two physicians and paid Matt to defend them. He copied the Fund, the agency that provided the statutory $1,000,000 excess layer of coverage for each medical provider. He copied Juan, Marc, and Beth at Leeds and included Jim's demand letter and Jim's expert reports. Matt also summarized his telephone conversations with his own consultants and requested any further insight anyone had on obtaining favorable expert review from a reputable OB specializing in high-risk pregnancies. He jotted a handwritten note on a blind copy he sent by fax to John, "Talk tomorrow in Mexico."

Matt did not reveal to anyone anything about his suspicions regarding Derek Sommer. Matt would defer that until after Derek's deposition and the completion of Matt's preliminary investigation. He did not want to risk being told to stop his investigation, and he felt no compulsion to respond to Jim's settlement demand at this time or at that level. He understood the medical issues and was well aware of the financial stakes, but for now he planned to try the case rather than settle it. He said good night to Andrea and went home to pack for Akumal.

CHAPTER 13

"It'll be a little over an hour to Akumal," Matt said. "No radio, but at least the AC's working great. I know you're used to your S-Class, John, but Mexico is the only place they still make these VW Beetles, and I think it adds to the adventure."

Matt and John agreed on the plane not to talk about the Sommer case until they were home, so Matt played tour guide on the way south from the Cancún airport to the white archway turnoff to Akumal. As he pulled past the Super Chomak grocery store on the right, Matt pointed to the structure on the left with the sign above the thatched porch roof saying, "Mini Super Las Palmas." "Chomak is the tourist version, and Las Palmas is for the locals and any tourists who dare. We'll come back for a drink at the palapa bar on the beach and stock up on groceries after we unload," Matt explained.

Matt pointed out the dive shop and some of the newer restaurants on the way back the rough road, paying attention not to hit the huge speed bumps too hard or at the wrong angle in the overloaded Beetle. He pulled off on the right under a sign, "Casa Tortuga," and pointed at the pink series of rounded two-story towers and entranceways. "We're in number 3, on the left."

"Bring your stuff," Matt said. "You guys can be upstairs. It's bigger and will give you some privacy."

"Oh my god, John." The balcony hot tub came into Lindsey's view as she looked around upstairs. "Look at our hot tub, honey." John passed by Lindsey as he went out on the balcony, and she called down from the top of the stairs, "You can come up and use our hot tub anytime, Matt. Let me change and we can get in some beach time before we go back for whatever."

*****

At the end of a restful afternoon, they piled into the Beetle with their tops over their bathing suits and headed back to the palapa bar of the Lol Ha restaurant. After two rounds of margaritas with warm nacho chips, two kinds of ceviche, a mixed Yucatán platter, and some tacos carnitas, with loads of fresh guacamole, they were all satisfied and able to finally check out both grocery stores and stock up on tequila, rum, mixers, Coke, and beer.

Everyone was tired and a little drunk, but it was only 9:30 when they got back to the villa. "Can you make a nightcap margarita with all that stuff, boys?" Lindsey asked. "I say we relax out in the hot tub. Gotta pee first, then I'll fill it up."

Matt was surprised, when he and John returned with the drinks, that Lindsey was not already in the hot tub. It was full and bubbling relentlessly, but she was still organizing towels beside her shirt, which was already on the chair, and turning the balcony light on and off.

"Better off. There's a nice moon," she said. Lindsey unhooked her top and let it fall forward as she leaned down, looping her thumbs into each side of her bottom and pushing it as far as necessary until gravity took over—all in one movement. As she stood erect, she turned toward the tub and stepped in. She did not turn back until she slid into the seat and the frothy water covered her front to about the same height as her top had.

When John and Matt got in the water, Matt realized the advantage of sitting across from Lindsey instead of at her side. She shifted back in the seat to make room for Matt, which lifted her breasts to the top of the fluctuating waterline, where they were held and jostled randomly with the buoyancy of the warm, air-filled water.

"We forgot our drinks," Lindsey said. "Be a doll, Matt. Can you get them?"

You've got to be kidding! Matt checked his excitement as he stood and calmly retrieved the margaritas. He placed one on the blue ceramic deck of the hot tub by each of their places. Just as casually, he leaned and fell backward into the tub. The water pushed over John and Lindsey as their body parts mingled. The ice was broken. The mood was set. And there didn't appear to be any rules.

*****

Sunday was a restful day, with the most exertion being moving the sunbathing operation from the pool to the beach after lunch and a couple of beers. Lindsey's bikini was bright red, and when she set up to tan her front when she moved to the beach for the afternoon, she put the top in her bag. Matt wondered for an instant what Brenda would look like in that red bikini with her lithe, even younger body and her auburn hair.

Monday was an exploration of the Mayan ruins at Tulum. The real attraction of Tulum was the cliffside setting overlooking the azure Caribbean Sea and the inlet beach below.

Tuesday, they all went to the local Yal-Ku lagoon, which Matt knew was less commercialized than the cruise line preference, Xel Ha, and you could see more fish more clearly. Matt's favorite was the colorful parrot fish with its mouth pursed like their namesake birds and able to crunch through the coral to feed. When he circled back to show John and Lindsey, he saw her tight, muscular legs flaring wide from their origin, marked by a thin patch of royal-blue bikini, and kicking seductively along the surface of the water. They ended the day with a trip into lively Playa del Carmen. As the trio strolled Fifth Street, the vendors beckoned to John and his wife of thirty years, "Hello, honeymooners. Come and see. No charge to look. Everything is almost free today. Come on in, honeymooners."

They kept the snorkeling gear through the following afternoon and swam out from the villa to explore Half Moon Bay to the live coral reef that extended all the way across to Cozumel. When they tired of the effort, John offered to return the gear to the dive shop. He said he would get some more Negra Modelo and another bottle of Herradura tequila reposada. Lindsey suggested a walk, and Matt joined her south to Akumal Bay, where they thought they might see

John, and then farther on to Jade Bay when they didn't. When they returned to the villa, John still wasn't back. Lindsey took off her top, lay down on her stomach, and turned halfway up to Matt.

"My neck is killing me from holding my head up while we were snorkeling. Could you rub me a little, please, Matt?"

"Sure." Matt wondered if he responded too quickly. He put some extra suntan oil into his palms and started to knead Lindsey's shoulders, back, and neck. He allowed his hands to drop off her back, just to the point that the feel of her ribs under his fingers gave way to the fullness of the sides of her breasts as she lay pressing on them. He kept looking back toward the villa for John to arrive and practiced what he would say. Before John returned, Matt realized Lindsey was asleep.

At the Lol Ha that night, they were midway through the main course when Matt felt Lindsey's foot hook around his calf under the table and start to rub up and down. There was no question this was intentional. Lindsey looked up over her mango margarita glass while increasing the pressure of the arch of her foot against the back of Matt's calf.

"Thanks again for the massage today, Matt."

John didn't bite, and Matt didn't want to be the first responder.

"My neck was sore from snorkeling," Lindsey said in John's direction. "Where did you go all afternoon, anyway?"

"I was talking to the guys at the dive shop about fishing," John said. "I can get them to take me out over the reef toward Cozumel and then down in the direction of Belize for a full day for half of what it would cost me back at Ocean City."

"You should do it. Take Matt with you," Lindsey said as she scooped her top down enough in the front to show both of them that there was already very little distinction in skin color where her tan line had been. "I'll keep working on my tan."

John still was not biting. "We'll see. Maybe Friday."

That night, everyone was more quiet than usual in the hot tub. Matt was still self-conscious about the massage, even though his imagination was more damning than reality, but Lindsey rubbing up against his leg at dinner was real, and he didn't know what to make of it. He wondered what John was thinking about everything.

CHAPTER 14

Lindsey came down early the next morning wearing, as far as Matt could tell without staring, nothing but one of John's red golf shirts.

"John's really out of it. Are we on any schedule today?" Lindsey dragged her feet as she walked.

"Not really. We'll go up to Cancún if you still feel like it. Want coffee? We can sit outside."

"Sure, thanks."

"You okay?" Matt said.

"Do you miss Dana?" She shuffled closer to him when he smiled. "I miss my life with the girls sometimes."

"Come get some coffee. Want it Mexican?"

"Just give me a hug."

Matt pulled her close.

"What're you doing with my wife?" John said from the stairs.

"I'm giving her a hug," Matt said.

"Okay. Don't wrinkle my shirt."

Matt released Lindsey. "Coffee?"

"Sure. Didn't sleep so well last night. Shouldn't have had that cup after dinner. That Mexican shit is tough. No wonder they put so much cream and sugar in it." John opened the slider to the porch for all of them to exit. "Still up for Cancún?"

*****

As soon as the Beetle came off the Hotel Zone exit and passed the park, Matt pointed out the Club Med. John and Lindsey expressed amazement at the density of hotels from that point on. Matt continued up Kulkukan Boulevard all the way to the point past the Camino Real, and then inland along the bay as far as the El Presidente. Matt wanted them to see the only three hotels that existed when Matt was first there in the seventies.

He doubled back to the Hilton, where he was able to wrangle a day pass for the pool and beach because of the Hilton Honors program on his American Express card. The arrangements were made with a young woman with thick black hair about as long and straight as her miniskirt. Matt considered asking her to join them for dinner, but she would not pass his cardinal rule for dating women only older than Dana. As she turned away, her long legs punctuating the movement of her constrained hips, her three-inch heels clicked on the marble floor, confirming her place in Matt's might-have-been mental scrapbook.

They capped their day with dinner at Lorenzillo's, watching the sun set at a deck table overlooking Nichupte Lagoon. The only problem with their specialty, Caribbean lobster, was that they had no claws. You had to get one big enough to fill up on the tail meat, which was expensive, by the pound.

"You know, Matt," John said, pulling at his signature lobster bib tied loosely around his neck, "I thought about picking up all your meals since you paid for the flight and the villa, but hell, the way you eat, it'd cost me more that way."

"Not to be a downer, but tomorrow's our last day, boys. What do you want to do?" Lindsey said.

"Well," John said, "I made plans to go fishing all day, like I said, and I know you won't go, and Matt's been talking about Coba all week. Why don't you take Lindsey, Matt? Sounds like she'd love it."

That night in the hot tub, Lindsey was excited about their jungle adventure. It seemed to Matt that she was finding reasons to sit up out of the water, get in and out of the tub, and have her legs and hands casually rest against various parts of Matt's body under the water. He started to get excited about the Coba trip as well. He wondered why John planned it that way.

*****

Matt dropped John off at the dive shop early Friday morning, and he and Lindsey kept going down toward Tulum and then back through the jungle for another hour. The road to Coba was a two-lane with no shoulders. They passed dirty children partially clothed carrying water buckets from common wells, fires burning outside open huts furnished only with hammocks, and chickens, dogs, and pigs running loose across the road. There were enormous speed bumps that were extremely effective. An occasional man rode by on a bicycle, with a machete or a rifle slung over his shoulder. Six-foot-long thick green snakes were sunning themselves at territorial intervals on the stove-hot road surface. Lindsey was chatty, which Matt took as nervousness for their safety.

The name Coba means "ruffled waters," referring to the many lakes in the vicinity. Matt suggested a guide to Lindsey, and this was the first thing they learned. Coba was not marked as well as Tulum and was not fully excavated like Chichén Itzá, so it was harder to identify the ball court, or the planetarium, or the hall of kings. Even the largest pyramid, Nohoch Mul, was open only on one side and was fully encased in vegetation and partially buried on the other three sides.

The guide deposited them back at the entrance and lingered for a tip. Matt drove Lindsey to the center of the little village and then back the dirt road to the lagoon for a late lunch at Club Med Villas Arqueologicas Coba Hotel.

"Let's look around," Lindsey said when they finished their lunch with a glass of well-chilled wine.

They walked through the arch into the courtyard. She stopped suddenly, inhaled audibly, and commented on the beauty of the trees and vine arbors surrounding the pool. The back of Matt's hand brushed against hers, and she curled her fingers into his. This time, Matt made the move. He turned to her. He looked directly in her eyes until their lips touched, and then he pulled her tight. Lindsey brought her hands to his arms, and Matt waited to feel whether she would use that position to push him back or to pull him tighter still.

He held on her lips in a tender push, and then he felt her pull him, ever so slightly; and he opened his mouth. Lindsey pushed her fingers into the hair on the back of his head, clutching it, releasing it. She pulled her hands down each side of his spine, scratching deeply through his shirt, and then tucking half their length down inside the waist of his shorts.

At the first sign of Lindsey's response, Matt angled her out away from him on his left and brought his left hand up along the fitted side panel of her shirt and across her right breast. He felt the soft, full flesh give under the increasing pressure of his sweating palm. Her bra was thin, and Matt could make out a lace design as his fingers crested over her nipple and spread out in every direction.

Lindsey pressed herself against Matt as he hardened in throbbing pulsations. She pulled her chest back, as if to suggest for Matt to move his hand across to her left breast as well. Matt slid his hand inside her shirt at the open neck, the top button unfastened against the force of his forearm. He pulled his hand back over the lace surface, noting the response of her nipple, and then placed it back around her naked breast by slipping under her bra this time. Lindsey pulled her hands back up to Matt's arms, and he waited for the signal.

She didn't push him away. She simply squeezed Matt's arms above the elbows and withdrew her tongue. Matt knew he had to stop, and he did. Immediately, he restored his hands to holding Lindsey from the back, and they stared silently into each other's eyes.

They held hands back to the car and drove without speaking for the first half-hour.

"Linds, what am I supposed to do with this? Forget it? Apologize? Forget you?"

"Don't forget it. And please never forget me. I don't want you to feel sorry about anything." She paused. "I don't know. Put it in a box, like, on a shelf, where you can find it, and get it back down again. Someday."

Another hour passed in painful silence. After taking the Akumal exit, Matt pulled over at the Super Chomak parking lot.

"You remember that night during our second year of college? I drove you home, and you asked me why we never stayed together."

"Matt, honestly, you remember the silliest things from back then. I never asked you that."

"Yeah, you did. And we talked about it. And now I'm asking you again. Are we ever going to be together?"

"Yes" was all Lindsey needed to say and all Matt needed to hear.

*****

Over a margarita, John excitedly told Matt and Lindsey about the fish that were caught and the ones that lived to swim another day. The captain of the small boat kept the fish that were good to eat, and John tipped him for making it such a memorable day. Lindsey shared what she could about the excitement of her Coba adventure with Matt and suggested they drive to Playa del Carmen for the evening.

The feeling that was Playa took over as they walked, and the heat and the light of the sun gave way to the heat and light of night in a party town. After the first call of "Hey, honeymooners," Lindsey took both John and Matt by the hand, pulling them in an awkward and hesitant gait. The next vendor called out, boldly following them up the street from in front of his intricately carved gourd lanterns and brightly colored cord hammocks, "Hey, threesome! Hey, special deal for you today. Three for the price of two. Ha, ha, ha. Come on in, honeymooners. Hey, threesome!"

*****

"No hot tub tonight, boys," Lindsey said as she led them to the door of *Numero Tres*, Casa Tortuga. "I'm too tired."

Matt said good night and undressed for bed himself. He looked at his back in the long mirror framed in a pounded-tin design. Four red scratches streamed down each side of his spine, and eight distinct welts blossomed across the top of his buttocks. Matt smiled to realize why Lindsey didn't want to end their stay with the nightly ritual of the hot tub. He fell asleep calmly and quickly, with every sense of his being absorbed in the memory of the soft warmth of Lindsey's breasts under his hand.

*****

Isla Mujeras, off the tip of Cancún, is the easternmost point of all of Mexico. The sun rises first over the Island of Women and arcs west to create the longest sunbathed days of Cancún. That was one of the factors considered by those responsible for the development of the Riviera Maya as a premier international resort destination. One consideration beyond quantification in constructing the equation for the perfect vacation was, the personal demons each of the millions of tourists who would flock to this Caribbean paradise would import from every corner of every culture in the world.

Matt remembered from the American novel course he took that Hemingway's first was initially titled *Fiesta*. He couldn't remember if he ever learned the reason the author or his publisher changed the name to *The Sun Also Rises*, but Matt thought the characters and the story were far too complex and certainly not happy enough to be described as a fiesta.

Their plane lifted and turned out over the jungle of Quintana Roo. Matt looked across the aisle at John quietly reading his book and Lindsey flipping the pages of her magazine. He thought that somewhere out there, a little deeper inland and farther west, where the sun was headed, was Coba. They had come for the fiesta that was Cancún, but as the sun also rose on that particular Saturday morning, the English translation of the archeological site that was home of the single excavated triangle of Nohoch Mul pyramid better described their not-so-perfect vacation in paradise. Matt knew he had drawn his friends John and Lindsey into ruffled waters. Matt leaned back into his seat, wondering if their friendship would ever survive this trip.

CHAPTER 15

Matt expected to ease back into his office routine by preparing for the deposition of Derek Sommer. After he greeted Sandy and told Andrea what he could about his trip to Mexico, Andrea told him the deposition was just postponed until the first week of March. Matt went over where Andrea was on her investigation. There was nothing else she could do until Matt questioned Derek at his deposition.

"Well, we'll just have to wait until March." Matt reached for his calendar. "Why couldn't we do it in February?"

"You have the trial in Pottsville."

"Right." Matt opened the Sommer discovery file. "Jim prepared all these responses himself. Why isn't he seeing what we're thinking?"

"I'm not sure I see what you're thinking either. Yet."

Sandy came into Matt's office and announced that Dr. Little was there to see him. "He seems agitated," Sandy said. "I'll bring him right up?"

Moments later, John strode through the doorway, outpacing Sandy's five-foot, two-inch frame. John closed the door behind him, cutting Sandy off.

"Hey, John, good to see you." Matt came from behind his desk. "Ready to talk about those expert reports?"

"No." He paced to and from the window on the far side of Matt's desk. "No. I...uh, I finished a delivery early and just started walking up the river. Until I got here. I...uh, I just have to get this off my chest."

Matt sat against the front edge of his desk. "What's up, man?"

"Matt, you can't let this thing with Lindsey go any further."

Matt didn't know what John knew. "Well, if you've talked with Lindsey, then you already know she didn't let it go any further." *This time.*

"I haven't talked with Lindsey at all. I'm talking to you."

"Listen, this thing with Lindsey, it is what it is. I don't know what I can do about it."

"I've known you've had this thing between you for over forty years. You and she can feel whatever you want for each other. I know I can't stop that." John now stood directly in front of Matt. "What I'm asking you, here...now, is that you don't take it any further."

Matt processed without speaking.

"You'd always tell me about this woman, and the next one," John said, filling the silence, "and I listened. I was supportive. As your friend. I should have been honest and told you it was wrong, and that's on me. I watched what it did to your marriage. It almost killed Dana, you know, when you left. And for what?"

John circled around the guest chair and put his hands on the back. "There were consequences, Matt. You were married. Hell, some of *them* were married. They had kids!" John lifted the chair from the back and slammed it down. "Lindsey's married too. She's married to me, for Christ's sake."

Leaning hard into the back of the chair, he continued, "We grew up, Matt. We're not talking about high school pickups anymore." John moved back to the window. "Seriously, how do you just take what you want without thinking about the consequences?"

The words flew out before his thoughts were formed. "I don't know. It's so easy sometimes. I just do it because I can." Matt looked John hard in the eye when he turned back from the window. Matt clenched the muscles of his jaw against whatever was going to happen next. "Just like you, John. You took what you wanted when you wanted it because you could."

They stared indefinitely without moving. Matt knew this was what he wanted to say to John for three decades. And he knew it was still the wrong thing to say to John.

"So there it is." John advanced toward Matt, and Matt gripped the edge of his desk in anticipation. "Okay, Matt, here's the deal. You don't have a trial expert yet in Sommer, right?"

His grip relaxed. "Right."

"Well, I'll write your damn report, and I'll come to the trial, and I'll testify. Jim Newman won't get a hint of concern out of me about the Swan-Ganz. I'll cover everybody, and I'll throw it all back on the Sommers, medically, for what happened when they refused admission. I'll have the jury wondering how she ever could have died after I support all the decisions those guys made at Leeds." John went to the window again.

"And what?"

"And you don't do anything to move this thing you have with my wife, whatever it has been, whatever it is, whatever it has to be. You." He faced Matt. "You don't take it any further."

So that's the deal? But Lindsey said we would be together. "Okay, John, but not because you made it a deal. I have more respect for you and a hell of a lot more for Lindsey than that." Matt stood up, not knowing if they were going to shake hands. "You have my word."

They did not shake hands. John left with the same pace he entered. Andrea came in after she saw him pass and asked Matt what that was all about.

"Dr. Little came to tell me he changed his mind. He's going to do the Sommer's expert report and testify at trial."

"I thought he never did that. He just did informal reviews. That was the deal. How did you convince him?"

Matt thought about the medical chief executive officer at Leeds, who was often criticized by his operational and financial staff for not doing a more formal strategic business plan for the growth and management of the complex, multi-institutional health-care system. Dr. Clark would lean down into the microphone, and in that trademark low and gravelly voice, he would look around the room, holding everyone's attention with a long silence, and respond, "We may not do a lot of planning, but we rarely miss an opportunity."

"Dr. Little created an opportunity. I just took advantage of it." Matt smiled as Andrea shook her head and walked out of his office.

Matt thought again about his last prom dance with Lindsey, before John took what he wanted. And now Matt gave John his word.

Matt corrected the PAMIC trial report on the Sommer case to read, "Defense Expert, John Little, MD."

CHAPTER 16

Two weeks later, Matt pulled in along the medieval-fortress-look-ing gray courthouse of the Twenty-First Judicial District in Pottsville, the county seat of Schuylkill County, Pennsylvania, to park in the back lot for attorneys. The trial of the pregnant young woman who died with her fetus of septic shock from a paper cut on the tip of her finger started as predicted. Matt represented the general surgeon, Dr. Retief. The ER physician and the admitting internist were also named as defendants, along with the hospital.

The woman was first sent home from the ER, then when she came back with her finger inflamed with infection, she was admitted but not referred to Dr. Retief for two days. In that time, the swelling in her arm from the infection created a compartment syndrome that cut off the blood flow before Dr. Retief could open it surgically and relieve the pressure and debride the dead tissue. By then, it was too late. Septic shock shut down all her body systems in expected order, and the fetus was too young to deliver.

Plaintiff's attorney, Paul Cappelli, demanded full policy limits for all defendants. By the time the plaintiff's case closed on the third day, Eric Britton arrived as the claims representative of the Fund. During a break in the trial, he circled all four defense counsels in the hallway.

"Cappelli's demand is way too high right now." Eric's youth and inexperience did not help him sell his analysis to the four sea-soned and successful trial attorneys he addressed. "We need to stick together to gain some leverage once the defense case starts if we're going to be able to settle this case."

Physicians have the right to refuse to give consent to a settle-ment under the terms of their primary malpractice insurance policy, and without that consent and an offer of the primary limit to the Fund to negotiate a settlement on behalf of that physician, the Fund could not override that lack of consent and force a financial contribution. Dr. Retief did not give his consent to settle. He did not believe he did anything wrong and all the negligence occurred among the other providers before he was even consulted. And by then the tragic end result was predetermined for this young woman and her unborn child.

"Well, nothing's changed since the defense meeting at the Fund a month ago," Matt said. "My guy won't consent, so we aren't going to settle together. You're new at the Fund, but you have to know the Fund isn't my client. My client is the doctor. If Dr. Retief doesn't want to consent, I'm sure as hell not going to push him because it would make your life easier. You better be thinking of a different settlement strategy that doesn't involve contribution by me and is still based on not pointing fingers among these defendants. That's the best strategy no matter what, and we all know it."

"I told you before, Matt, the Fund wants this case settled for all defendants, and Dr. Retief has to consent to achieve that global settlement, with equal contribution on behalf of all defendants by the Fund."

"What you really mean is that his primary carrier has to put up the two hundred thousand limit so the Fund has two hundred thousand less to have to pay for a global settlement." Matt looked around at the other counsel. "You don't have to waste my time trying to bullshit me. I've been doing this for as long as you've been alive."

"However you want to look at it, Matt, but it doesn't appear to the Fund that you are cooperating with the agreed-upon defense strategy."

"Doesn't appear to who at the Fund? Have them call me. Get them on the phone right now and we'll talk this through."

Eric's pear-shaped head seemed unstable atop his pear-shaped torso, but he didn't move.

"I didn't think so. No consent, Eric, and no money. You want to settle, get it from these other guys. You want to sabotage the trial with finger-pointing? Go ahead. You'll just feed into Cappelli's hand

and pay more. And Retief will still walk." Matt realized he was now fighting Cappelli, the other defendants, and the Fund.

When Matt reported to the courtroom in the morning, Paul Cappelli was in a plaid sport coat. Matt now knew the case had settled. Paul was too astute a trial lawyer to wear a plaid sport coat to cross-examine the defendants. The jury would not take him seriously in that outfit. Eric tried to keep the details of the settlement by the other defendants from Matt, but Paul told Matt the settlement amount.

Matt walked back to the hotel to pack and checked out earlier than expected. As he came out of the hotel to get his car, he saw Paul coming up the street with his partners for lunch at the hotel restaurant.

"Congratulations, Matt! Hell of a job getting out of that one without paying a penny."

"Don't congratulate me," Matt laughed. "You're the one with all the money."

"Yeah, but none of it's yours, buddy."

"Here." Matt pulled all the change out of his left pants pocket. "What's this? Here, eighty-five cents. That's my contribution." Matt held out his hand. "With what that settlement netted you in fees, that would make your take about six hundred thousand dollars and eighty-five cents." Paul actually took the change. "You're a local boy. You ought to be able to buy a Yuengling somewhere for that here in the home of America's oldest brewery."

"I can get two Yuenglings for that back at the office. I always keep some in the fridge. Want one? On me?"

"Can't do it, my friend. Another time." Matt could not afford to be seen having a drink with the plaintiff's counsel on the last day of trial.

"Seriously, Paul." Matt extended his hand. "You did a great job trying a rough case. It was a pleasure to watch."

"I'll get you next time, buddy." Paul shook Matt's hand and went with his partners to celebrate.

"Paid jacket was a nice touch!" Matt called after them. Paul's high-pitched laugh faded as the two adversaries walked in opposite directions.

Matt slid into his black Audi and started back to Harrisburg. He thought he might want to celebrate too. After all, Retief got away without paying anything to be dismissed from the case. He stopped for a hot turkey sandwich in Frackville before getting on 81 instead because he wasn't sure how he wanted to celebrate or what he wanted to celebrate or with whom he wanted to celebrate. Fighting with everyone every day was tiring.

Once back in the car, he got a call from Rick Dalton at the Fund. Rick was claims manager at the Fund in large part because of Matt's recommendation when the director called Matt for his opinion. They didn't always agree on the approach or the value of a case, but they had a mutual respect that stood the test of many professional disagreements.

"Eric tells me you were not very cooperative during this case with Cappelli."

"Oh yeah? What did he say I did or didn't do?"

"He sent me a memo before trial alerting me to your lack of cooperation during the defense meeting, and he documented the trial file with memos about how you were acting independent and against the interests of the Fund. He told me, when he called for final authority that night, that it cost more because of your failure to cooperate in the settlement."

"Bullshit, Rick. I did my job for my client, even when everyone else started pointing fingers. Retief had a defensible position, a good expert, and every right to refuse to consent. Eric lost control of this case because his pride was hurt when I wouldn't do what he wanted. He let everybody throw sand in the sandbox, and now he can't figure out how they all got dirty."

"Okay. I get it. We're good. I just needed to hear it from you."

"Thanks. You know you'll always get a direct answer from me."

"And you would have gotten one from me if I didn't like what I heard." Rick hesitated. "Hey, you ever follow up with Brenda Warren? Looked like you two really hit it off after the presentation."

Matt flashed to his vision of her in Lindsey's red bathing suit. "Why, you jealous?" Matt responded quicker than he should have.

"No, I've been away and on trial. You're right, though, I should check in with her to see if I can be helpful."

"Yeah, that's what I meant, for sure. You really are a piece of work."

When they hung up, Matt thought about Brenda again. She stepped out of her fitted business suit and into that bright-red bikini. *I promised John. Maybe it is time to give Brenda a call. Right after Derek Sommer's deposition.*

CHAPTER 17

Sandy came into Matt's office on the day of the deposition and announced that Attorney Newman and his client were in the conference room and the court reporter was set up. Matt took his briefcase, packed with what he needed, and walked downstairs to start the testimony of Derek Sommer, MD. Derek was thin and physically fit. He sat erect. His blond hair was well-trimmed and blown dry. He looked too confident. After the professional courtesies and the preliminary instructions, Matt decided to see if he could make the good doctor uncomfortable right from the beginning.

"Are you married, Doctor?"

"Now?"

"Yes, now. Are you currently married now, Doctor?"

"Yes."

"And your wife's name?"

"Harriet."

"Her full name, please, Doctor?"

"Harriet Franklin Sommer."

"When did you get remarried to Harriet Franklin?"

"February 15, 2009."

"That was, what, about six months after your first wife died?"

"That's right."

"When did you meet Harriet Franklin?"

"Objection," Jim stated for the record as he put his hand on Derek's arm. "Direct him not to answer." The reporter took down every word.

"Discovery deposition, Jim. All objections are preserved for trial. I'm not sure how this could be relevant until I have the answer." Matt anticipated Jim's basis for the objection.

"Next question," Jim said.

"How long did you know Harriet Franklin before you married her?"

"Objection. Next question," Jim said.

"So I guess you'll object to a line of questions about how well he knew her in medical school or during his residency at Brooklyn Memorial and whether he ever visited her in the house where they now live together?" Matt did not get a reaction from Jim.

"Derek, Attorney Morgan seems to be concerned with how quickly you remarried after Lisa's death. Tell him why you did." Jim turned from his client to Matt. "Maybe we can save you some time this way."

"I decided I couldn't stay at Leeds after Lisa died. I needed a change. I went back to where I knew people. My baby needed a mother. I started seeing Harriet after I moved back to Brooklyn, and she was only working part-time, and it was easier than trying to meet someone new." Derek was certainly no romantic.

"All right, Doctor, let's talk about this life insurance policy you identified in your interrogatory answers. When did you put that in place?"

"Objection to the form of the question," Jim said to protect the record with the only objection that was not preserved to the time of trial. "You can answer, Derek."

If Matt did not change the question, he ran the risk of having the answer stricken if the deposition testimony was used at trial. Matt accepted that risk and waited for the answer.

"Lisa and I talked about it as soon as she knew she was pregnant. She was a working professional, and she wanted insurance on her just like I had on me in case the baby needed anything if something happened to either one of us."

"How did you determine to insure Lisa's life for two million dollars?"

"That was what the agent said was appropriate for her income and life expectancy."

"Whose idea was it for Lisa to continue to work at the ICU during her pregnancy?"

"What do you mean? That was her job. Of course, she would keep doing her job until she had to stop."

How arrogant. What a pompous ass. How could she have stayed with this man? "How about on the seventeenth," Matt asked, "when Dr. Alvarez and Dr. O'Bannon recommended that she stop and be admitted for the duration of her pregnancy?"

"What's the question?" Jim said.

Matt leaned in, staring at Derek. "Why didn't Lisa follow her physicians' advice, if he knows?"

"Do you understand the question, Derek?" Jim protected the record and gave his client time, but the question was clear enough.

"Yes. Lisa wanted to keep working. She loved her job at the ICU, and she didn't think they could get along without her."

"What about you? What did you think?"

"What I thought wasn't important, Attorney Morgan, you know that. Lisa was a competent adult, and I didn't have any right to say what she should do. Our expert witness addressed that issue, I think, in his report."

"Oh, I do know, Doctor, but didn't you express your opinion to your wife on that day that you needed her to take care of things at the house, take care of you, Dr. Sommer?"

"I don't remember that. She did take care of the house, and me. That was what she wanted as my wife, and she was able to do that even though she worked as a nurse."

"Was that your expectation of her? Was that your wife's cultural background?"

"Objection," Jim said for the reporter's benefit. "Direct him not to answer."

"I don't know, Attorney Morgan," Derek answered anyway, "but I don't think Lisa's cultural background is proper questioning. I remember one of your presentations to the medical staff that any inquiry into race or ethnic background was illegal."

"Okay, Derek," Jim said. "I objected to the question. Mr. Morgan will move on."

"Dr. Sommer," Matt said, "you're a cardiologist. Surely, you understood the medicine involved and the risks to your wife from preeclampsia?"

"Yes, of course, I did. And so did she."

"Well, from the seventeenth to the twenty-second, did you know her blood pressure levels, her urine protein levels? Did you take them? Did she tell you what they were? Did you see them?"

"Objection. Compound question." Jim leaned his chair back, lifting the front legs off the floor.

Matt went forward like he was connected to Jim by a rope. "Let's break it down, Doctor. Did you personally see any values in that time frame?"

"No."

"Did she tell you what they were?"

"I'm sure she did from time to time, but I don't remember."

"Did you care?"

"Objection—"

"Of course—"

"Move on, Matt," Jim said.

Derek seemed agitated now, despite Jim's consummate preparation. "Dr. Sommer, did you ever advise your wife to stop working and be admitted for observation and monitoring?"

"No."

"Did she ever tell you she wanted to between the seventeenth and the twenty-second, before she called you from home?" Matt did not wait for an answer. "In that time frame, did she ever tell you she wanted to stop working in the ICU and be admitted for observation and monitoring?"

"No."

"After the two of you met with the doctors on the seventeenth, did the two of you ever discuss what the risks of preeclampsia were, or the risks of progressing into eclampsia?"

"No."

"Never discussed that? A cardiologist and an ICU charge nurse in preeclampsia, pregnant with their first child?"

"No."

"Doctor, you never attended any of your wife's prenatal visits until the seventeenth, correct?" Matt pulled the prenatal record form his file, just in case.

"That's correct."

"Why did you attend on that date?"

"Lisa was concerned with her weight gain and her blood pressure, and frankly, I didn't trust Dr. Alvarez."

"What do you mean? Why didn't you trust him? Personally or as a resident physician or what?" Matt said.

"Both. I think he had become inappropriately personal with Lisa, and I knew he had some legal problems, from the talk around Leeds."

"How do you mean 'inappropriately personal'?"

"He was very friendly with her at our house." Derek shifted his weight. "And she talked about him a lot. It was apparent they had become friendly."

"Well, he was invited to your house for the resident reception over the fourth, right?"

"Yes."

"Were you aware of any other time they were together in a personal or social setting?"

"No." Derek shifted back. "Not that I was aware of."

"Dr. Sommer, did you ever confront your wife about your concerns regarding Dr. Alvarez?"

"Objection. Direct him not to answer."

Jim let this line of questioning go on longer than Matt expected, but Matt didn't want Jim to think he had to stop now. "He opened the door, Jim. I'm just trying to understand his testimony."

"Move on, Matt. This is not a relevant line of inquiry. He answered your question on why he came to the visit on the seventeenth. Next question."

"Did you trust Dr. O'Bannon, the chairman of the department?" Matt said.

"Yes, I had a lot of respect for him, before this."

"Then why didn't you follow his advice to have your wife admitted on the seventeenth?"

"I already told you, Attorney Morgan, and asking the question a different way won't change the answer. Like our expert stated in his report, I didn't have any ethical, legal, or medical right to consent for my wife."

"What did you talk about with your wife when you were alone in the room while Dr. Alvarez went out for Dr. O'Bannon?"

"Instruct him not to answer the question," Jim said for the record. "Objection to the form."

"That might be one we'll have to revisit with a judge, Jim. Could you mark that question, please?" Matt indicated to the stenographer. "Did you observe your wife crying at any time while you were alone with her in that room?"

"Sure, she was crying then. She knew she would have a difficult time with her pregnancy, but she was the one who decided not to be admitted."

"What did she say about that while you were alone?"

Derek looked at Jim, who nodded for him to answer. "'I have too much to do,' she said. 'I have too much to do to go into the hospital for the next two months.' She said she'd talk to her supervisor at the ICU in a couple weeks if her condition did not improve."

"Doctor, we sort of got ahead of ourselves. Let's go back to the beginning." Matt relaxed in his chair and pulled the rest of his notes in front of him.

They reviewed Derek's background, education, and training, then moved to the scope of his duties at Leeds, and now at Brooklyn Memorial. Matt asked about the health of the baby and then doubled back to Lisa's prenatal visits and inpatient chart, making sure what Derek knew and when about her condition. Matt asked Derek for everything he remembered being said by Juan, Marc, the ICU intensivists, the consulting cardiologist, and all the nurses. Matt then returned to the concern for Juan's inappropriate personal connection with Lisa and explored Derek's recollection of everything Juan said or did in his presence.

Matt covered all the damage angles before he turned the witness over to his own attorney. He knew Jim would have no questions, obviously not wanting to provide Matt with any more information than he had to. Matt knew he struck a chord of concern in Derek, but he certainly did not have a smoking gun. He would need to have Andrea work her magic and keep plugging away with the investigation.

"By the way, Doctor, why did your wife call you to come home for her rather than go straight to the ER, or call 911, if you know?" It was an afterthought, but Matt had never understood why Lisa did that.

"She wanted me to be with her, and she was not in distress anymore."

"What was her condition when you arrived home?"

"Comfortable, concerned for her fall, but as I said, in no acute distress." Derek hesitated. "She just had bad allergies."

"Did you provide any treatment to her before taking her to the hospital?"

"No, she didn't need anything at that time. I just wanted to make sure she was checked out thoroughly." Derek hesitated again. "I might have given her some medication to make her more comfortable with her allergy symptoms."

"What medication did you give her?"

"I honestly don't remember. Some generic, probably."

Matt remembered the case he had that involved pseudoephedrine and what he learned. *I wonder.*

*****

When Matt returned to his office after the deposition, he told Andrea to serve all the subpoenas for the phone records and the supplemental request for production of documents on Jim for Derek's own phone records. Matt then dictated the cover letter to Jim serving the defense expert report of John Little, MD, which he wanted Jim to receive at the same time as his copy of all the other investigation materials.

John kept his word and produced a stinging indictment of the irresponsible decision of the Sommers. He added a harsh and well-supported challenge to the plaintiffs' expert reports, complete with citation footnotes to journals, texts, and ACOG bulletins. John logically and methodically laid out his reasoning that the clinical management at Leeds was not only appropriate and within the standard of care but was also an example of excellence in responding to a difficult and predictable medical emergency resulting from failure of the patient to follow the instructions of her physicians.

John left open the defense that Lisa died from the progressive and insidious effects of her disease process, which were not exacerbated by the actions or inactions of the defendants. John concluded, as he must to comply with the standard for experts in Pennsylvania, that his opinion was stated to a reasonable degree of medical certainty. John's credentials were indeed impressive, and his report was exactly what Matt needed to gain some leverage with Jim.

All Matt needed now was the smoking gun connecting Derek to Harriet Franklin during his marriage to Lisa. Proving that Derek intended to endanger Lisa. Or worse. He would allow Andrea to conduct her investigation. He would look into his random thought about pseudoephedrine himself.

CHAPTER 18

The next morning, Matt drove south out of Harrisburg on Interstate 81 to the Route 233 exit southwest toward Pine Grove Furnace. About halfway between Laurel Lake and the road up over Big Flat to Shippensburg, at the line marker between Adams and Cumberland Counties, was an unmarked pull-off on the right.

Matt found the trail that follows Tumbling Run, a clear, spring-fed mountain stream rippling over an iron-rich bed and cascading across limestone shelves. He saw the orange "Private Preserve—No Trespassing" signs he had ignored for thirty years and focused on the mature stand of hemlocks, the state tree of Pennsylvania, and mountain laurel, the state flower, that flanked the creek. Michaux State Forest was home to all the natural beauty that kept Matt in Pennsylvania. This morning, before the laurel was yet in bloom, Matt thought about all the times he had come here with Linda, with Dana in a carrier pack, and later when she could handle the climb on her own, and everyone special in his life—except Lindsey.

Matt kept his obsession with Lindsey passive and largely dormant during his married years. Until things deteriorated with Linda. *Lindsey showed the first interest,* Matt convinced himself in order to justify their affair three years ago. He responded then because he could. Matt replayed their nights together when he hit the place where the trail veered almost indiscernibly off, up and to the right over exposed roots and rocks through dense vegetation. Copperheads and timber rattlers inhabited these rocks and rejuvenated their life-essential heat by sunning in the paths. The sense of imminent danger matched the adrenaline rush that he felt making love with Lindsey while they were both married.

Matt climbed to Lewis Rocks, a cluster of huge granite boulders lifted and placed by the movement of the underlying shelf that thrust the Appalachian mountain chain upward from the earth and the push and withdrawal of the glacier that repositioned everything in its path over the surface of the earth. He sat atop the highest of the vertical rocks, looking out over both sides of the valley. In the peace of his favorite place in the world, Matt thought about bringing Lindsey here, and of all the other ways they could be together like Lindsey said. If they were together. But they weren't. They couldn't be. Because he gave his word to John.

All the way down the path, paying attention not to slip on the wet rocks and leaves, Matt felt himself let go of the pain and longing that fueled his Lindsey obsession. By the time he saw his Audi through the trees and across the log bridge, he thought that maybe he would finally call Brenda.

*****

That night was quiet at Qui's. Matt sipped a fine Meursault and polished off his hand-rolled gnocchi with hearty Spanish and Italian sausages and broccoli rabe. Elide went to bring his Santiago tort, the dense lemon and almond creation that she made from her mother's Brazilian recipe and pulled for him fresh from the oven. Matt stopped Staci, thanked her for a great wine recommendation, and asked if he could borrow her cell phone quickly. He knew she had an unlisted number.

"Sorry to bother you, but I left mine at the office, and I have to check something before I get home"

"No problem, hon. Here." Staci always moved at a hundred miles an hour and continued to the next table.

Matt dialed. He shielded the mouthpiece as much as he could to look like he was talking.

"Lindsey Little," Lindsey answered. "Hello. Hello, anybody there?" Lindsey hesitated in response to Matt's silence. "I can't hear you. Must be a bad connection. Call me back."

Matt closed the phone when Lindsey hung up. He struggled for a breath. *Goodbye, Lindsey.*

He handed the phone back to Staci. "Thanks again. Nobody's home."

"Sure, hon. You're welcome. We all done here?" Staci stacked the plates.

"Yeah," Matt said. "Afraid so."

The waitress brought the check and the signature chocolate pebbles. Matt had an account and just signed his name and left a tip in cash. He said goodbye to Rosemarie "Qui Qui" Musarra, who came out of the kitchen for the ritual departure, and headed out. He turned up Green Street, minding the uneven brick sidewalk after the wine. He pulled out his own cell phone. He could wait until he got home, but he wanted to do this now, before he changed his mind. He scrolled down to the new number he stored two months ago and pressed to call. He stopped and leaned against the streetlight at Briggs so he wouldn't be out of breath and sound like he was walking.

"Hello."

"Hi, Brenda, this is Matt Morgan. We met at the governor's presentation to the medical society."

"Oh, I remember you, Attorney Morgan."

"That was a good idea—get ahead of the changes to the Fund with the medical community. You made a nice presentation." Matt envisioned her that night in her stylish deep-burgundy pinstripe business suit, and a black lace camisole low across her ample freckled cleavage.

"Thank you." Brenda's tone was light and whimsical, betraying the ongoing focus on business issues. "I am sure you would like to see some more changes."

"Well, yes." Matt was still trying to find a way to make the transition he needed to make. "I'm not sure the ones you've planned will be enough, but it's a start. I understand you will be personally responsible for making it all happen. Good luck with that."

"Thanks," Brenda said. "I suppose you have some ideas on what else could be done, counselor."

"Sure, if you ever want the perspectives of a litigator in the trenches, I'd be happy to share them." *It's time.* Now Matt's tone changed also. "But I...uh...I'm calling on a personal note."

"I thought you might be, at eight thirty at night, to my home number."

"I also understand that you're not in a committed relationship right now."

"That was right two months ago, when I gave you this number. Is this cross-examination from the trenches?"

"Well, if that's still the case, and...uh...no, this is not cross-examination. But I wondered whether you'd like to get together for dinner sometime." Matt was rusty, but he wasn't showing Brenda anything he didn't want her to see—just like in the courtroom.

"That was why I gave you this number. Two months ago. What do you have in mind?"

"Do you know Mangia Qui?" Matt said.

"Sure. We go there all the time from the hill. Mostly at lunch, though."

"That's why I haven't run into you there. I'm kind of a regular for dinner. I live in the neighborhood."

"You told me you lived in the historic district. You know, when we met eight weeks ago."

"Sorry it's taken a while. I've been in court and traveling around on cases. Anyway, are you available this Saturday?"

"No, actually." Matt was not expecting that answer. "I'm going to be away for ten days, visiting my brother in DC for Easter."

"I thought your brother was a DA in Brooklyn." Matt feigned confusion to gain time.

"One of them is. This one's the US attorney in DC, remember? It's only been two months since we had this conversation. Early Alzheimer's?" Brenda had made her point. "Be back the following week, though. That work for you?"

"Great. Would you like me to pick you up, or do you want to meet at Qui's?"

"Let's just meet at the restaurant and see how it goes from there."

"Good choice. I am about two dateless weekends away from becoming a stalker."

"No, I didn't mean it like—well, yes, I did. But I didn't mean to offend. I just don't know you very well. I have heard some pretty good things, though, which also makes me skeptical."

"Another wise choice. Stay away from the nice guys with the good reputations," Matt said. "You really are a hard case."

"Save your closing argument for dinner. I'll meet you there at eight."

"Good. I'll look forward to it, if I can remember." Matt enjoyed a good fight. "Have a nice Easter."

"You too. Doing anything special?"

"My daughter will be around."

"She doesn't come with a wife, does she?"

"No, not anymore."

*****

The illumination of the Capitol dome created a halo effect through the light rain starting to swirl in the night air. Matt watched from the lamppost, feeling the drops ease down his face as if to wash away all his past and cleanse him for whatever his future would hold. And then, as the rain worsened, the weight of the wasted life of Lisa Sommer came over him. When he turned toward his house, he knew he had to get to Derek. And destroy him.

Matt was intrigued by the hunt. He stopped hunting small game when his father became too ill. But in his day his father could walk farther and longer than Matt hunting through a sorghum patch, a stand of cornstalks, or a tangle of mountain laurel—even in the hard rain. Matt wanted to hunt Derek now. He remembered the rush when a proud and beautiful bird started abruptly, trying to avoid the unknown stalker who controlled its fate, and in the process startled the surprised hunter with a flush of adrenaline.

He's mine.

CHAPTER 19

On Monday, Andrea went into Matt's office as soon as she saw him park in the lot behind the office. She laid the phone records across the front of his desk, facing his chair, and pointed to them as soon as Matt walked into the office.

"I think I've got something you can use." Andrea watched as Matt circled to his chair. "Dr. Sommer's records weren't complete from his house or his cell. He didn't have anything too far back, according to his answer, and the records from Harriet Franklin didn't show anything I recognized. At least she had all her records, though." Andrea pointed to that stack.

"So what do you have that's good?"

"Well, look at this. The records from the cardiology department at Leeds and the records from the anesthesia department at Brooklyn Memorial have some matching numbers."

"Whoa. Show me." Matt came around to the front of the desk so Andrea did not have to read upside down. He sat with Andrea in the two burgundy leather guest chairs. She turned the records toward them.

"See, this number from Leeds is to Brooklyn, and it repeats all through here." Andrea ran her finger up and down over the months following the death of Lisa Sommer until the date Derek left Leeds. "And over here," she added, pulling the records from Brooklyn Memorial closer, "this number from Brooklyn is to Leeds. See?" She turned to Matt. "There aren't as many, but they're spaced over the same time."

Matt pulled back in his chair and looked straight at Andrea with his best pleading-puppy face. "Anything before Lisa died?"

"Yep. Nothing from Brooklyn, but here," Andrea responded, beaming as she pointed, "are four calls from Leeds to Brooklyn, July 6, August 18, and two on August 22."

"And that is the number for the anesthesia department at Brooklyn Memorial Hospital? You're sure?"

"Yep. I called them when we served the subpoena. They didn't have to reply to a Pennsylvania subpoena, but they agreed to get everything ready if we provided a subpoena issued in New York under the Uniform Act. I worked through your lawyer friend up there, and by the time we had everything to them, they sent us their records the next day. We matched the numbers with the records we already got from Leeds, and there's no question those calls were made from where Dr. Sommer worked to where Harriet Franklin worked."

"Any way we can match an extension to Derek personally?"

"No. This is a general department number the calls were made from."

"How about in Brooklyn? Any way to tie the receiving number directly to Harriet?"

"No. General number for the department there too."

"Damn. Okay, and nothing from either of their home phones to each other during any of this period?"

"Nothing that I could see. But, Matt, Dr. Sommer called her before his wife died. Isn't that the smoking gun you were looking for?"

Matt stood up and placed the records side by side and studied them. He knew Andrea was thorough, but this was so close he had to be sure. How could he confirm it?

"It's still circumstantial, but the first one was the day of the office visit right after the Fourth of July party where Juan was at their house and Derek was jealous or suspicious or something." Matt laid his pointer finger on the next date. "This one was right after they refused admission, and on the twenty-second." Matt moved his finger down. "Let's see the times. One was probably before he went home for Lisa, and the other one would have been right after she died. That son of a bitch!"

"What can we do with this if it's only circumstantial?"

"Make a discovery response package of these. Highlight the matches and do a cover letter serving the results of our subpoenas on Newman. As soon as possible. Very factual. No conclusions, no drama. Then set up a meeting with Elizabeth Burns at Leeds, George Peterman at PAMIC, and Rick Dalton at the Fund. I want it here, and I know it's Easter weekend coming up, but I want it this week. We'll hold off on talking to the doctors until the folks with the money decide what they want to do with this." Matt's thoughts were moving faster than he could give his instructions to Andrea.

"Do you really think Dr. Sommer did something to his wife?"

"I do. Or he didn't do something for his wife. Point is, he let her die just the same. And he had a reason in Brooklyn. And two million more reasons."

By that afternoon, the meeting was set up for Thursday in Matt's office. By that evening, Matt had the smoking gun.

"Bob, this is Matt Morgan," Matt told the pharmacist over the phone. Bob Larson worked with Matt in the earlier case where the young boy stole the pseudoephedrine from behind the counter at Leeds, swallowed a handful, and ended up shooting his best friend with a shotgun that his father left unattended in the house. Because it contained the main ingredient for the illegal manufacture of methamphetamine, pseudoephedrine was now kept behind the pharmacy counter, quantities were limited by federal regulation, and records of all sales were maintained. "I need you to check some records for me," Matt told the pharmacist. "I'm working on another case for Leeds, and I need to know if any pseudoephedrine was sold on August 22, back in 2008. Might be useful in my defense of Leeds."

Bob didn't hesitate to respond to Matt's inquiry. The records were maintained electronically and organized and cross-referenced by date, drug name, physician prescribing, and purchaser so that reports could be sent to the feds at any time. And Bob knew Matt's longtime connection as defense counsel for Leeds. "Only one that day, Matt. Dr. Derek Sommer ordered it—for himself—and paid for it. Picked it up that day."

"Thanks, Bob, that's all I need for now." Matt meant it. That was all he needed. Pseudoephedrine, used as is and not for the manufacture of illegal drugs, acts as a vasoconstrictor to shrink the blood vessels. It is used for a runny nose because it minimizes mucous production and dries up nasal drainage. Matt also knew that vaso-constriction would spike even a normal person's blood pressure and increase their heart rate. It could account for why Lisa's blood pressure could not be controlled at Leeds once she progressed to eclampsia. If Derek gave it to her.

CHAPTER 20

When Thursday arrived, Matt set his coffee in front of his prepared materials and greeted Elizabeth, Walter, and Rick, who were already seated around his cherry conference table. Matt confirmed that they were all there to decide on a trial or settlement strategy for the Sommer case. Matt reviewed the plaintiffs' settlement demand, summarized the plaintiffs' expert reports, and estimated the damages resulting from the death of Lisa Sommer. He reiterated the position of Dr. O'Bannon and John Little, MD, essentially that she would have died anyway and the real negligence was in the patient's refusing admission on the seventeenth. Matt admitted the factual issues for the jury and recognized clear exposure on the medical issues presented by the experts. If the case went south, Matt concluded, the verdict could exceed all the available PAMIC insurance coverage and expose the excess coverage from the Fund and, ultimately, the assets of Leeds.

"What do you recommend?" Elizabeth asked since Matt had not included any recommendation in his preliminary reports.

"I really brought you all here to discuss an alternate theory of this case, Beth." Matt shuffled his papers for effect. "It is my theory, which I can support with these results of discovery and my investigation, that Lisa Sommer's decision to refuse admission on the seventeenth, which we now know was critical to her course, was driven by her culturally submissive allegiance to her husband. Dr. Sommer, a cardiologist, knew the dangers of her condition all too well and may have deliberately planned for that condition to progress to her detriment, and possible death." Matt surveyed the room for any reaction. He saw none. Yet.

"He had renewed a personal contact with a woman he knew from his residency while Lisa was alive. He married this woman, Harriet Franklin, within six months of Lisa's death. And by the way, he took out a two-million-dollar life insurance policy on Lisa when she became pregnant."

"Wait a minute, Matt." Rick beat Beth to the punch. "What the hell are you—"

"You can't possibly be serious?" Beth said. George remained silent in the face of his largest client taking her position.

"Listen, there's more." Matt chose to talk directly to Beth, but he did not plan to tell them everything. Not yet. "Derek complained of some kind of personal relationship developing between Lisa and Juan Alvarez, who was her primary OB. We have phone records establishing contact between Derek and Harriet between July and the date Lisa died, and—"

"That's why Andrea asked for our phone records?" Beth said.

"We asked for them in discovery from Derek and got them from Brooklyn Memorial and Harriet by subpoena to the provider." Matt nodded, never taking his eyes from Beth. "And yes, that's why we got yours, from the cardiology department, to compare the numbers. And we got four hits with Brooklyn."

"There could be a hundred reasons someone contacted that number, and even if it was Dr. Sommer contacting this Franklin woman, maybe they were all friends." Rick had the most financial risk if the case did go south.

"So Attorney Newman knows about this discovery and the subpoenas?" Beth drilled her elbows into the beautiful redwood.

"Yes, and I think we can gain some leverage with Jim with this because I don't think he is getting along too well with Derek."

"Matt," Beth said, clasping her fingers, "do you know what could happen with this in the press if we're wrong? Dammit, Matt, do you know what could happen with the press even if we're right? He was our doc too. You're going to implicate him in this thing based on... on what? Some records of interdepartmental phone calls? Some... some insurance proceeds they got when they were having their first child together? Is that it? This is really going to sell papers because of some Hispanic sexist loyalty thing, for God's sake."

No, dammit, there's more. "Beth, in context, this all adds up. The medicine is good here, but Lisa died. She died in childbirth at Leeds. That doesn't happen anymore. We have to have something, or we might as well write a blank check. And this is it—the leverage we need to win this case." *And destroy Derek Sommer.*

"Win it?" Rick laughed. "Correct me if I'm wrong here, Beth, but I'm not hearing 'Try the case,' Matt. What do you think, Beth? Two limits?"

"If we can even get it for two million and four hundred thousand dollars." Beth composed herself, looking at George, adding the PAMIC primary layer of two hundred thousand and the Fund excess coverage of one million for each defendant. "If we consent on both docs, are you okay?"

"Sure," George said. "I don't see this as a Leeds exposure." Leeds would have an additional 1.2 million dollars also.

Matt never expected anything but agreement with Beth from George.

"There you are, Matt," Rick said. "Two limits. Can you do it for that?"

"Subject to board approval," Beth said.

"And subject to our claims committee approval," George said.

"Okay, if you get approval for two limits, can you do it for that?" Rick said.

"Matt, if Jim already knows about all this, okay, if he knows, he knows. You can use this theory for leverage if it works, but do not—and I repeat, Matt, do not—push this thing or take it public in any way. Understand?" Beth sounded like she wasn't even sure she wanted Matt to be the one to pursue negotiations.

"Yeah, okay. Two limits is enough, Beth. And I understand. Will you call me to confirm?" Matt did not want to settle, but he knew if these people holding the purse strings did want to settle, this approach would help. He didn't have to argue or try to convince this group today.

"Of course. George, call me back, too, when you get authority. And you'll call Rick?" Beth spoke to George directly.

"Sure. Sounds like a plan," George said.

Matt watched George and Beth walk out together first, studiously considering all that Matt said. Matt gathered his papers, knowing what he hadn't said. Rick collected the coffee cups.

Rick laughed softly and shook his head. "You really are one crazy son of a bitch." He walked to the conference room door. "You know that?"

"Yeah, but I won't spend all your money. Wait and see." Matt reached out and pulled at Rick's sleeve. "Tell you what? You give me 40 percent, just like Newman's going to get, you give me 40 percent of the difference between two million and four hundred thousand and whatever I get it settled for. How about that?"

"Crazy son of a bitch! I wish I could, my friend, I wish I could."

"Come on, put your money where your mouth is, Rick." Matt let go of Rick's sleeve.

"By the way," Rick said, "you call Brenda yet?"

"Yeah, I called her. Not sure what'll come of it, though. She wasn't available."

"You're losing your touch, old man." Rick held his cupped hands out in front of his chest and nodded, taunting Matt about Brenda's ample figure.

"You wish," Matt said.

Rick continued out the door, mumbling past the reception desk, "Crazy son of a bitch."

CHAPTER 21

The message was "Hi, Daddy. I'm going to be with Mom for Easter. Sorry. Call me." Matt understood and did not want that fight. Not now. He set the cruise control as soon as the speed limit on 81 north out of Harrisburg changed to sixty-five. Matt made the trip to New York City in under three hours. He needed to get away after the meeting and after Dana's message. He respected Dana's decision, and he respected Linda. He made the last-minute reservation at the Hilton on Sixth Avenue between Fifty-Third and Fifty-Fourth. There was nothing to keep him home this weekend.

Out of the Holland Tunnel, Matt went out Canal Street through the bustle of Chinatown. He crossed the Manhattan Bridge and wound his way into the alphabet streets of Brooklyn. He turned onto G Street and pulled up in front of 1253.

The woman was short and thin, with blond hair under a bandanna. She was playing with the young boy of three or so, who sported a colorful shirt under a baseball cap. The boy's face seemed darker than hers, but it could have been the shadow from the cap. They laughed and kicked a soccer ball, and then the woman picked the boy up in her arms and hugged him all the way into the house.

She turned at the last minute, like she was expecting someone, but she was not looking in Matt's direction. Matt walked to the front door of the house directly across the street, checked his watch, and rang the bell.

"Good morning. Is Dr. Sommer home?"

"You've got the wrong side of the street, mister. Dr. Sommer lives over there." The woman was holding her plaid robe closed with one hand and pointing with the other.

"Wow. How long has he lived over there? I always thought this was his house," Matt said.

"Well, I don't know exactly. On and off ten years or so, I guess. There was a time he wasn't around much, but with the boy, it's been, what? About three years now." The woman was still talking to Matt through the storm door.

"This was where he lived during med school, right?" Matt scratched his head like he was performing in a sitcom.

"No. Dr. Sommer never lived here. The Franklins always lived across the street, and that was when Dr. Sommer, in med school, that was when he started living with the Franklin girl."

"Okay, well, that's how I got confused. When he left after school, do you know where he was then?" Matt looked across the street to confirm that no one was out.

"No, you'd see him coming or going, but it wasn't till a year or so before he came with the boy that he was here more often."

"What do you mean 'came with the boy'?" Matt said. "I didn't know he had a child."

"Well, he's adopted, you know. Harriet never was pregnant, not that anyone could tell—she's so skinny—and then they were all just here together."

Matt heard the red Porsche Carrera before he saw it pull into the driveway across the street. "Okay, well, by the way, what is your name, ma'am?"

"There he is now. Dr. Sommer. He's just now getting home from the hospital. No other cars like that on this block!" She laughed. Matt nodded and raised his eyebrows to her.

"Ethel Harris. Ethel is my name."

"Well, thank you very much, Mrs. Harris. You've been very helpful." Matt's heart rate jumped to see the cardiologist come from his driveway toward Matt.

"Attorney Morgan." Derek increased his pace. "Attorney, do you want something? What are you doing here at my home?"

"I can't talk to you without your counsel—"

"Didn't your doctors do enough? They killed my wife. What are you doing here?"

"Really, Dr. Sommer, I can't talk to you."

"Your doctors killed her. Alvarez—"

"Ethically, I'm not—"

"They killed—"

"I'm not allowed—"

"Get out! Get out of here! You all killed her!"

Matt reached his car. He knew he could get in now even if Derek acted on his anger. Derek was in his face, and Matt clenched his jaw before he relaxed into it. "No, *you* killed her, Dr. Sommer."

Derek stopped.

"You killed your wife."

Ethel Harris stood in her doorway when Matt slid into the Audi and pulled away from Derek Sommer standing alone in the street.

Matt took the Brooklyn Bridge instead back into Manhattan. *It was worth it. To cross that line. I shouldn't have confronted Derek. It will give Jim a chance to prepare. To get ready for me.* "And it was unethical," he said out loud. But now he had Ethel. And the pills.

*****

Matt returned his car to the Hilton and checked in. He walked south down Broadway, angling across midtown Manhattan to the Village, then straightening out south of Houston between Soho and Little Italy, lost in thought. He turned right before he hit Tribeca to feel the excitement of Canal, then back up West Broadway to the Latin bistro he enjoyed. A Black man with lots of body art across his rippling muscles and a headband holding back dreadlocks, exposing a large single wooden embedded earring, prepared and served Matt's first mojito. The young man busied himself filling the next order, and the barmaid came from the kitchen with an early dinner for the couple sitting next to Matt at the bar.

"Hi, I'm Elissa. Let me know when you're ready for another," she said after she served the couple their meals, and turned her attention to focus on Matt. "You waiting for anyone?"

"No, thanks, Elissa. Just me tonight."

"I'll get you some chips."

Matt remembered the plantain chips with corn relish salsa, and he wasted no time digging in when Elissa returned. "Thanks. I'll take another when you get a chance. No hurry."

"Okay, hon." Elissa smiled at Matt like she knew him, and the warmth of her voice fit the white stucco Latin motif Matt took in by reflection in the mirror behind the bar.

She was probably Hispanic, but Matt detected no hint of an accent. Her skin was light golden brown, and her curly hair was tinted with tones of yellow and red as it swept back from her face to a festive silk tie. The ends dropped in foot-long strands over her shoulders. Her plain white top scooped at the neck and was stretched tight across her chest, shaping her small breasts through the crepe material tucked into a long full multicolored skirt. Her smile pushed her cheeks out and up, and her forehead narrowed at her hairline. Her nose, which gave away her mixed-race heritage, flared with her smile as well, creating a friendly glow that was not hardened by the rigors of her job.

"Like a menu?" Elissa served the second mojito to Matt, who was looking over at the grilled fish and pork chop plates in front of his neighbors at the bar.

"Sure, might as well. I may be here for a while."

The small dining area filled up as the salsa band set up in the corner. Matt reflected on his trip to Brooklyn that afternoon. He took comfort only in that little Louis seemed comfortable with the only mother he had ever known. Matt pulled hard on the mojito, drawing the rum up from the bottom through the thick, muddled mint leaves, and shook his head as he looked over the menu. *I had to go. But I shouldn't have.*

"I'll have the short ribs, please, and another mojito, when you get a chance—"

"I know. No hurry." She tossed her hair as she lifted away with the menu.

Elissa moved with a fluid grace in her arms, sweeping the glass from the shelf, pouring from the bottle, and mixing the liquid ingredients over ice. When she worked the long wooden mortar to grind the fresh mint, Matt realized the breadth of her shoulders and the strength of her arms. She was thin, and against the backdrop of the bottles shelved in front of the mirror, he realized how tall she was. He had a hard time with this age, but he figured she would pass his test and was at least five to ten years older than Dana. He let his eyes droop from her smile when she came back with his drink, looking past the glass to the white crepe tight to her body.

Two bites into the ribs, Elissa leaned on the counter, resting her cheeks in her hands, elbows propped on either side of Matt's plate. "How are they?"

"Great." Matt assumed she was talking about the short ribs. "I've had them before. They're really tender."

"Yeah, I know. I get them all the time. Here on business?"

"No, not really. Just playing."

"That's a nice sweater." She pulled back, took the pencil from behind her ear and the pad from her hip, and moved to the far end of the bar to take the order of the two guys who just sat down. "Enjoy," she called over her near shoulder. Her hips swayed, moving the long full skirt in waves from her waist to her thong leather sandals.

Matt's black zipper sweater was a gift from Dana, and it did make him look younger. Not young enough to handle Elissa, he thought when she returned.

Elissa resumed her pose and cocked her head to the side as she spoke. "So what's your name, Mr. Mojito?"

"Matt." He smiled and extended his hand, causing her to lift to the left to take it. Her hands were surprisingly warm and soft. He came back with all he could think of. "Have you worked here long?"

"Couple months. It keeps my days free, you know."

Matt assumed, like most aspiring actresses and models, she needed to be available during the day, but she still needed to eat when she didn't have work. "I'm just here for the weekend, but this is one of my favorite places, so I'll be back."

"So, Matt, I only work till ten tonight. You want to get a coffee somewhere later?"

Matt realized he never let go of her hand. He squeezed gently and, in a one-sided smile, replied in an unusually lower voice, "I'd love to. I'll be right here when you're ready."

They talked through the next hour and a half, while the band played and the other patrons danced. Matt had one more mojito. He couldn't wait for the time to pass. He thought only once about Brenda, and not at all about Lindsey. His stomach churned, sending a tingling sensation through his groin and down his legs. The music stopped, the band packed up, and the hour approached. Elissa came out from the back wrapped in a long loose-fitting blue cape with her hair tucked up into a large rimless hat that fell over to one side with the weight of it.

"Where's the best coffee?" Matt ushered her through the front door, past the smoker's bench.

She turned to him, holding both his hands and leaning in. "I don't want coffee."

"Well, should we get a cab? I'm up at the Hilton, midtown. Maybe we could find a drink up there."

"I don't want a drink either." She leaned further into him. "Or a cab." She was an inch from his face with hers, and at her height their lips were almost touching. "Or a hotel." She dropped one hand, turned down toward the triangle below Canal, and summoned him. "Come with me."

They entered her small studio off Avenue of the Americas, past where Walker ends, sparsely decorated with an Ikea flair. She threw her cape and hat over the only lounge chair as they passed it. She turned on no lights or music, and without a word, she pulled her top off in one cross-armed movement, revealing her naked body in the light spilling in from the street. She pulled Matt to her in a kiss that lasted while she unzipped his sweater and pushed it back over his shoulders onto the floor. The night became early morning, with Elissa's long legs wrapped around him, her chest damp with the effort of their pleasure.

*****

Matt took a cab to the hotel, and the sadness set in. No one was hurt, and there were no expectations, but this was why he didn't like casual sex. He could not relax into pleasure for its own sake. His passions could be triggered like any other man's, but he wanted it to mean something. He struggled with the emotional aftermath of his night with Elissa for a while longer. He showered, packed, checked out, and headed down the West Side Highway before the Sunday-morning city was awake. By the time he was out of the Holland Tunnel and headed out 78 for home, he concluded that the pleasure of Elissa was worth the pain of walking away from her bed at four o'clock in the morning. It was only then that he wondered what pleasure would come from his call to Brenda.

CHAPTER 22

"Hello, this is Matt Morgan." Matt always answered his own phone.

"Good morning, Matt. This is Walt Pendleton." Matt recognized his deep voice but wasn't expecting to hear back from the executive vice president of Leeds. "Hope you had a nice Easter."

"Yes, Walt, thanks." *I certainly did.* "How have you been?" Matt knew what the answer would be.

"Busy." Walt never disappointed. "This Sommer case is pretty bizarre. You know, I knew Derek when he was here. Never met Lisa. It's really tragic, especially for two of our own."

"So Beth briefed you on our meeting?"

"She did, but I wanted to hear what you really think. She glossed over some pretty strange stuff, about the calls, and suspicions about Derek, and…and I never heard anything like that from you before."

"What I really think is that Derek may have committed the perfect crime." Matt waited for a response, and in the silence, he continued, "He didn't shoot Lisa or stab her or strangle her. He never even touched her. That's the beauty of it. He let her own body destroy itself."

"Pretty strong accusations, Matt. What do you have?"

"He's a cardiologist. He's written articles on the systemic cardiovascular effects of hypoxic events at the cellular and molecular level. He knew what would happen to her in preeclampsia if she wasn't admitted, if she kept working in the ICU and at home. That disease is irreversible and progressive, and he controlled her. He controlled her and prevented her from making the decision she would have—should have—made on her own." Matt talked faster and faster, trying to review the evidence in an orderly fashion as though he were preparing for his closing argument.

"I understand it was legally her decision not to be admitted on the seventeenth. She was a competent adult, but O'Bannon and Alvarez saw them in that room together, Lisa crying, and Derek all puffed up about how she was indispensable and could monitor herself better in the hospital. Listen, Walt, it was classic cultural submission to his personal and professional position of authority, and he knew he could get away with it."

"We're not going to ride that horse—not the Hispanic effect."

Matt understood that Walt always had to think about the good of the system as a whole.

"Okay. Well, we also know about the phone calls to the woman he married less than six months after Lisa died. One was right after Derek first showed some concern about Alvarez having some inappropriate relationship with Lisa. One was after the decision not to be admitted on the seventeenth. And the final two are on the twenty-second—one before he even goes home to bring her to the hospital, for Christ's sake, and then again after she died. And then there's—"

"These calls," Walt said. "Aren't they just between hospital numbers? Do we know Derek actually made or received them?"

"No, not for sure. Not yet. Jim Newman didn't let Derek answer those questions, so we'd have to go to a judge to get a decision overruling the objection and instruction, and then ask Derek the questions again."

"If the judge lets you." Walt paused. "So we would have to create a public record of our theory to pursue the calls?"

"Yes, but I think the dominoes are in place. Listen, I have a witness. A neighbor I discovered after the meeting with Beth. I'll be able to prove Derek had physical contact throughout his marriage to Lisa with his current wife, Harriet Franklin. He lived with her in med school and during his residency, in Brooklyn, and they kept in touch all this time. And the last domino is the check for two million dollars of life insurance proceeds," Matt said. "When that falls, it's all over."

"Maybe, Matt, maybe. But it's not our style, and he was part of us—they both were. The board doesn't want to risk the press exposure. We have bigger fish to fry right now with all the acquisitions. PAMIC pays their two hundred thousand for each of our docs, the

Fund kicks in the million each, and our assets go to bigger and better things. You have authority from the board to settle, but I know the docs have to consent and PAMIC has to agree. Green light to get it done, at least from here." Walt continued when Matt did not speak. "For what it's worth to you personally or professionally, I and a few of the board members believe you might be on to something, but you have to stay away from it."

But I didn't tell you about the pseudoephedrine he used to spike her blood pressure. "Okay, Walt, I will." Matt knew it was already too late for that. "I'll talk to the physicians and let Beth know when I have consent and PAMIC is on board." *It's not my money. It's not my decision.* "Thanks for calling, Walt."

*****

Matt placed two calls and was able to talk personally with both Marc and Juan after clinic hours. Matt's portion of the conversation went pretty much the same with each of them. They both listened attentively while he laid out the plan for settlement. They asked very few questions. Matt did not address his own concerns about Derek and limited his discussion to the exposure to the two physicians from the unexplained and tragic death of Lisa Sommer.

"It isn't right, Matt," Marc said, "having to settle a case where you did everything right to save a girl's life, and her child's, and there wasn't any medicine in the world that would have made a difference." Marc's tone changed. "I guess we don't want to take that argument to the jury?"

"I've tried several cases to a jury where I knew they might find negligence, and my only argument was that it didn't matter to the outcome. In fact, I just won one like that earlier this year. But no, with the stakes this high, that's not a good gamble here."

"Okay. Do I need to sign anything?"

"Yeah. I'll have the form faxed to you in the morning. Andrea will call first. Thanks, Marc. I'll confirm when everything is resolved."

"I expect to be here another couple of weeks. Sort of figured this thing would wind up before summer. When I go out west, I don't plan to come back. I'll give Andrea my numbers. Thanks, Matt. I learned a lot from you."

"Thank you, Marc." Matt was sorry to see Marc leave Leeds. "I believe you, for what that's worth. No medicine in the world would have made a difference. Tough situation."

"Saddest day of my practice. That girl's life was just plain wasted."

*****

Andrea took care of all the paperwork the following morning, and Matt confirmed the physicians' consents to Beth at Leeds, and then to George at PAMIC. George called Matt back forty-five minutes later to confirm PAMIC's consent and that he tendered the two $200,000 primary insurance limits to Rick at the Fund. It was right before lunch that Matt heard back from Rick, confirming $1,000,000 authority for each of the two physicians, and giving Matt the go-ahead to proceed with negotiations with Jim Newman for a global settlement on behalf of all defendants within the total amount of $2,400,000.

Matt dictated the letter to Jim, setting out very little of the facts or the defense arguments, since all that had been set out before, and offering the plaintiffs $750,000. He stated that $400,000 would come from PAMIC and $350,000 would be contributed by the Fund. He made it clear that the defendants were not admitting liability or waiving the right to proceed to trial if the offer was refused.

Matt knew Jim would not accept anything like this amount, but by the same token it was not a nominal offer either, and Jim would have the ethical obligation to present it to his client. Matt instructed Sandy to fax the letter to Jim, and he went home for the day. It was not his money, and it was not his decision, but this was not how he wanted this to end. He did not want Derek to get away with wasting the life of Lisa Sommer.

CHAPTER 23

Matt listened to the two phone messages from Jim when he arrived at his office the next morning. One was from four thirty the day before, about an hour after Jim could have received the offer letter by fax, and the other was from eight o'clock earlier that morning. Matt returned the calls at eight fifteen.

"Morning, Jim."

"I just wanted to make sure you were serious with that offer before I talked with Derek."

"That was exactly what I was trying to convey, that we were taking settlement discussions seriously. The Fund originally wanted me to start at $200,000, with no Fund contribution."

"Well, that's par for the course, but let's get realistic."

"Works for me," Matt said. "I'd just as soon try this case."

"No, you don't want to try this case. This is the first time a mother died in childbirth at Leeds in fifteen years. My demand is reasonable, and you know it. This case could go through the roof. A jury isn't going to accept that my client's wife wasn't admitted on the seventeenth, and when she was admitted on the twenty-second, your hospital waited nine hours to take the baby."

"I know your position, Jim, and you know mine. Your client refused to allow his wife to be admitted on the seventeenth, when Dr. Alvarez recommended it, and our expert is prepared to defend the care on the twenty-second. I'll take my chances with a jury before I agree to pay you three and a half million dollars on this case."

"Well, the 750,000 dollars you offered in your letter was an insult." Matt and Jim continued the familiar dance. "I could probably talk my client into accepting two full coverage limits, but 2,400,000 is as far as I could go."

Matt smiled to himself, knowing that he already had authority for that amount. The case could settle, and now the sport was negotiating a better number for the sake of the game. The only question was how well Matt could lie.

"The bottom line is that I'm not going to let this case add to your million-dollar club membership. I'm serious." His tone changed to the way attorneys speak to one another when they know the other one doesn't want to hear what they are about to say but they are going to say it anyway. "I'll take this case to a jury with my expert, Dr. Little." *I paid a high-enough price to get him.* "Three-fourths of a million dollars is a lot of money. You know we could set up a structured settlement annuity package that would pay out in excess of three million dollars on that investment over time, even after your fees and some up-front money for your client. I'll recommend nine hundred thousand, if you tell me your client will take it."

Matt knew the silence meant that Jim was processing the obvious import of Matt's statement. Jim would never bid against himself in the same phone call.

"We're too far apart, Matt, and I don't have any authority from Derek. I haven't even talked with him about your first offer. I think it will make him angry, and I was hoping to hear something better from you before I called him."

"You just did. Let me know."

*****

Jim did not call back until Friday, midmorning. "I talked to Derek, and I worked on him to see if we could get this thing done, but you're not going to like his answer."

"I don't like *him*, so the only thing about his answer that I have to like is the number."

"Let's not get personal." Jim still did not mention anything about Matt's encounter with Derek in Brooklyn.

"Okay, what can you do?" Matt said.

"He won't come down below two million five, and frankly, you can tell the authorities at PAMIC or the Fund or Leeds or the docs, whoever is calling the shots, I wouldn't recommend anything below the two-million-four limits, anyway." Matt knew Jim was prepared to drop a lot further.

"You've got to get past me first, and I wouldn't recommend anything near that amount. I had trouble getting provisional authority for the nine hundred thousand," Matt lied. "I already told you it had to be under a million."

"Two million, five hundred thousand is the formal demand. That's a million below the first demand, and I hope everyone respects that kind of movement."

"If you want me to convey that demand, okay, I will. But you know me. I make one offer to set the range, and then the final offer, take it or leave it. You're out of the range, my friend, and we *will* try the case."

"Two and a half million, Matt. Let me know." If that was all the authority Jim had from Derek, he had to make the demand.

"Pay real close attention when I call you back. It may take a few days to pull everyone together, but I'll get back to you." Matt had no one to contact.

*****

Matt understood it was now out of his hands. His only job was to settle the case without blowing the negotiations. The numbers were already right. Matt was playing the game for himself now, to bring justice somehow, as he perceived it, for Lisa Sommer. But the more he punished Derek with a lower settlement, the more Matt bought the justice he sought for Lisa at the financial expense of their child.

He was being told to settle a case he wanted to try, to back off from a theory he believed, to feel badly that he was willing to pursue it to the detriment of Leeds and its reputation, and all because the money didn't matter to anyone. Money would make it go away. Money was the only currency to compensate an injured plaintiff or the family of a dead plaintiff. This was the standard stuff of every closing argument of every trial, but it only made any difference if it was somebody's money making the decision.

But it wasn't Matt's money. Matt couldn't afford to be wrong, either for himself or his clients. His passion for this case was just that, his own personal, private passion. It made him care, for the first time in a long time, about a result. Now he knew why he had become so cynical before, how he had become so hardened and cold, and it made him sad. He wasn't sad about Derek's loss, or even their son's, but he was sad about the death of Lisa. And he was sad, as a professional, that he let her in.

CHAPTER 24

Matt finished his pho and walked his provisions for the week from the Broad Street Market the three blocks to his house. He rarely missed the Saturday-morning ritual. He hadn't spoken with Brenda since they made the plan for dinner at Qui's that night, so he pulled her card from the shelf behind his kitchen phone and dialed.

"Hello."

"Hi, Brenda. This is Matt Morgan. How was your trip?"

"Oh, hi." Brenda took a hard breath. "I was on the elliptical. Sorry, out of breath."

"Want me to call back?" Matt envisioned her in a leotard, sweating under a headband.

"No. I was almost done, anyway." She exhaled just as hard. "So yeah, it was nice in DC. My other brother and his family came down as well. I don't see everyone together very often. We still on for tonight?"

"Yes, that was why I was calling. I just came from the market and didn't buy anything for tonight, so I was hoping I had the date right." Matt pulled a stout out of the refrigerator and opened it, sipping it as he talked. He didn't' try to manage pouring it into the frozen mug. "Remind me, the one in DC is with justice?"

"Yes, Ron."

"And what does your other brother do again?" Matt feigned confusion.

"Joe's a DA in Brooklyn."

"Well, I'm glad you had a nice Easter break. I've been wrapping up some things on my next case, so I'm looking forward to relaxing this weekend."

"What case is that?"

"It's quite a story, actually. One your whole family might be interested in." Matt took a long swallow of beer. "I'll fill you in tonight."

*****

When they met at Qui's, it was the first time they had seen each other in casual clothes. Brenda wore beige linen pants with her flowered silk top unbuttoned at the top to expose a tangerine camisole. Matt was pleased to stand on her arrival and welcome her to his table in front of Qui's crew. It was not the first time he had brought a woman there, but Staci always made it seem as though it was.

Matt enjoyed the attention and the view and the wine and the meal. He relaxed more than he expected he could. He listened to Brenda's story about her trip to DC. She filled him in on her progress with the Fund. When it was his turn, he told the story of Lisa Sommer and what he believed her husband had done.

"I'm going to talk to the DA in Leeds about the pills, to see if she wants to look into it further. But Derek's in Brooklyn now, so I'm not sure how jurisdiction works in criminal investigations. And then there's the insurance fraud angle, and the federal regulations on pseudoephedrine. Enough to go around for the whole Warren family of attorneys." He raised his wineglass to toast the possibilities.

"That is quite a story. Can you really get into all that in a medical malpractice case?"

"Well, I'm going to follow the evidence. My job is to defend Leeds and the docs, so whatever I have to do, I'm prepared to do. This was such a tragic loss of life. And I really don't think it was caused by any medical negligence."

"Let me know if any of us can be of any help." Brenda did not seem convinced to Matt. "I'm sure you don't need any help with your defense, though."

Matt checked his watch when he saw the restaurant clearing out. "Can I interest you in a nightcap? I'm just down the street."

"No, thanks." Brenda collected her purse. "I drove, and I need to keep my wits about me to get home tonight. Working for the governor and all."

"I'm not sure we ever got around to discussing anything about ourselves. I thought we could focus on our personal stories for a while."

"Yes, I'm not sure what this was either, a business meeting or a job interview, but let's save that for another time."

Matt flashed to the prom his junior year when he took Lindsey. Late at night, reclined on the couch after they got back to her house, he started to unbutton her blouse while they were kissing. Lindsey stopped him and asked what he was doing. "Unbuttoning your blouse," he told her.

"Well, let's save that for another time," she told him.

"Sure," Matt said to Brenda, shaking himself back to the present. "I'll walk you to your car."

Brenda approached her white Volvo SUV in Qui's parking area across the street. As Matt followed, he thought about how the "Good night" would go. At the driver's-side door, Brenda turned back to Matt in midsentence and kissed him lightly on the lips.

"How's that for personal?" She turned to open the door. "Good night, Matt. Thank you for dinner. Now you know my number works, give me a call." She eased into the seat with her hand on the door handle to pull it to her. "Or I'll call you."

Matt watched her back out and drive away down North Street, his insecurity compounded by the confusing goodbye. He was not ready to let her in. He was not ready to ruin another personal relationship. He was not sure he could make one work. But he wanted to. With this woman.

CHAPTER 25

"You know what I'm going to do with Derek." Matt moved from the Monday-afternoon introductory pleasantries with Jim. "I tried to get additional authority. I even talked with my people over the weekend." Matt was vague because it was not true. Legal negotiations were usually no more than practiced lying.

"No, I'm not sure I do, really," Jim said. "You don't have anything you can use at trial, so no, I don't."

"The jury isn't going to be very sympathetic to him, given his quick turnaround on wives, and those phone records will get me back in a deposition to find out just when he started that second relationship, which we all know was in medical school, and residency, and never ended."

"You really are full of yourself. You won't even get back to a deposition, let alone in front of a jury with that crap." Jim still had not ever mentioned Matt's confrontation with Derek in Brooklyn. "What are you trying to pull?"

"The real question is, What was Derek trying to pull? Don't forget about the two-million-dollar life insurance check he didn't waste any time cashing."

"Dammit, Matt. You can't believe that. I can't imagine Leeds is letting you do this. This'll backfire, I'm warning you."

"Warning *me*?" Matt was pushing him now just to push him. Part of the game. "Warning me about what?"

"This is unethical. This kind of accusation is irresponsible and unprofessional. Beyond zealous adversarial representation."

"Think about it, Jim, before you say anything you'll regret." Matt was still calm and methodical. "If I'm right and I prove your guy wanted this to happen to his wife, who's unethical? You filed the suit, and Derek signed the complaint."

"Let's both slow down before either one of us goes too far," Jim said. "You're a good trial attorney. I know that. I don't believe this thing for a minute, but if you get it in, you'll taint the jury. What's your number?"

"Taint the jury!" Matt said. "I've done that before. But this time I'll be telling them the truth." Matt swallowed hard and pursed his lips. "The truth is, he killed her. I don't have any number. No authority, no settlement. I'm ready to take my chances with the jury and get some justice at trial. For my clients. And for Lisa Sommer. I'm going to prove he killed her. I'll see you in court, Jim."

Matt did not slam the receiver into its base, but rather, he placed it with deliberate precision. He had initiated his plan, and he was at once both scared and relieved.

*****

Matt called PAMIC and the Fund first. He called Juan, Marc, and Beth. He lied. He told them he couldn't get the case settled within the $2,400,000 authority, and Jim was prepared to try the case. A pretrial conference was set for the first week in June, with trial to follow immediately. No, he told them, negotiations would not continue. He would prepare the case for trial and keep them informed. His last call was to John.

"Little residence."

"Oh, hey, Linds, it's Matt Morgan. I was calling for John."

"Matty, when are you going to stop introducing yourself when I answer the phone? You know, caller ID already tells me who it is, and I've recognized your voice on the phone for forty years."

Lindsey always treated him a little bit like a child, Matt thought. Probably because their relationship began as children.

"John's working late and on call. You can probably reach him at the office."

"Yeah, I thought I was calling the office, actually. Long day. Just wanted to talk with him about that death case he's been helping me with." Matt knew which number he dialed.

"Well, why don't you come over and have a drink with me? We can wait for John together, and then all play Scrabble or something."

"No, thanks, Linds. Not tonight. Rain check, though. I'll call him at the office. Don't drink too much by yourself."

"You know me. I only drink when I'm alone or with someone." She laughed, as she always did when she used that line. "So how about joining us for Memorial Day? We're going to have our usual pool opening party."

"Let me think about that one. Thanks."

"I'd like to see you, talk to you." Matt heard the clank of ice cubes in the glass as she took a drink. "Bring somebody, if you want."

"Okay, thanks. And we'll talk. After this trial, I promise."

"Love ya, Matty. Don't be a stranger."

*****

Matt pressed the button for another line and dialed John at the office. He was with a patient, and Matt left a detailed message on the machine. He told John he would be needed to testify as an expert in the Sommer case the first week in June.

It was too early for dinner at Mangia Qui, so he went to the Hilton to listen to Steve Rudolph on the piano. Matt walked to the far end of the bar and ordered a double Glenmorangie, straight up, to celebrate the initiation of his plan. He was prepared to destroy Derek Sommer—whatever the cost.

CHAPTER 26

Brenda did call Matt first. Matt invited her to hike the Tumbling Run trail, thinking that would be as far from any professional interaction as possible. He was right. That hike led to another day trip to the Gettysburg Bluegrass Festival. The third time they got back together, it was for dinner again at Qui's, and Brenda asked Matt to pick her up this time. She didn't want to have to drive home. When Matt opened the door for her to get into the Audi, she had a small bag in addition to her purse. When she put them both in the back seat, she looked straight at Matt.

"I don't need to be wooed." She kissed Matt as she steadied herself into the seat by placing her hand on Matt's thigh.

There was a lot of heat with Brenda, but not a lot of warmth. Matt's ulterior motives for pursuing her in the first place made him uncomfortable, but now he truly enjoyed his time with her. Under her auburn hair her toned alabaster body was covered in freckles. In his mind, Matt connected them in intricate patterns as they lay together naked. They both brought a certain detachment to bed, and their pleasure was measured in here and now. Matt didn't look for more than that because there wasn't complete honesty to begin with. He wanted that now but didn't know if it was too late. The strength of her youth was more than physical. Brenda was a player in the highest political circles. And her brothers could be helpful in Matt's plan.

She covered her breasts with the five-hundred-thread-count Egyptian cotton sheet. "I honestly never thought we'd end up here," she said.

"Thank God for scotch!" Matt said. He did not cover himself. "What did you want to tell me? Before?"

Brenda tossed the corner of the sheet over Matt's abdomen. "I was talking to Joe. They've opened a criminal investigation in Brooklyn. They'll coordinate with the DA in Leeds, and the feds on the pseudoephedrine. Ron's already looking into the insurance fraud angle, and they both said they'll cooperate with each other all the way through." She emptied the last of the scotch from her glass and placed it back on the nightstand. "That'll be the first time that's happened since Joe helped Ron build that snowman when he was eight."

"That's great." Matt reached for his glass, but there was no scotch left.

"That was what you wanted, right?"

"Sure, if it's there. If I can do anything, or if they need anything from Leeds, just have them let me know." Matt deliberately minimized the subject.

"Obviously, where they go will depend on how the trial comes out in two weeks. But I have faith in you, Attorney Morgan."

"I remember the first night you called me that." *And you told me about your brothers.* "If you're ever going to have faith in me, it should be in the courtroom," Matt said out loud again.

The first conversation Matt had with Brenda's brother Joe in Brooklyn and her brother Ron in DC, three weeks into their relationship, was to lay out the evidence he amassed against Derek. All the evidence, including that he purchased the pseudoephedrine on the way home to pick up Lisa after the first call to Harriet Franklin on the twenty-second. He shared all that with the DA in Leeds also. Now it looked like Matt would get what he wanted professionally—to destroy Derek and get justice for Lisa. He would not get what he wanted personally—not until he knew what it was.

"Oh, I have more faith in you than that." Brenda got up, brushed her teeth, changed into her nightgown, and crawled back into bed with Matt, facing the edge of the bed. He rolled toward her and gently put his arm over her shoulder, grabbed her hands at her chest, and pulled her gently into him.

"Good night."

*****

On one of their drives together, Matt pointed out John and Lindsey Little's house and told Brenda about the invitation to the Memorial Day pool party. He did not tell her anything more about Lindsey. In the morning, they drove north up Second Street, away from the already-gathering crowds for the riverfront holiday festivities. The Littles lived under the Blue Ridge Mountains in one of the older upper-scale developments for comfortable professional people. They bought the house early in John's career, and although they made some additions, it still held its original charm. The warm fieldstone and cream-colored-siding facade was fronted by mature shrubs and framed naturally by the wooded backdrop. The backyard was fenced, secluding the pool from the neighbor's view.

Lindsey answered the door in her red cotton shirt and blue shorts. Matt did call her back and accept her invitation, for himself and Brenda, but the look on her face made it seem like she didn't believe Matt would bring someone else to her house. She and Brenda were cordial, although Lindsey's affect appeared forced in the face of Brenda's unknowingly genuine greeting. Matt knew this could be awkward, but he was determined to move on with his life and embrace this last weekend of relaxation before he tried the Sommer case. He handed Lindsey his signature macaroni and cheese he made that morning, and Brenda offered to carry in the lemon sponge pie they bought at market on their way out of town.

The Little pool party was a study in simplicity. Everyone brought something to share, and Lindsey made a huge pan of baked sweet lima beans from her mother's recipe. John grilled hot dogs, hamburgers, and chicken basted in his secret marinade. He never divulged the ingredients, but Matt narrowed it down to a pretty closely proportioned facsimile of vinegar, oil, salt, pepper, celery seed, garlic, and onion when he tried it on his own. John also provided an iced assortment of beer from Troeg's Brewery in Harrisburg, and that was it.

The weather was perfect, the pool was clear and warm, and the guests were easy and open to accepting Brenda. Lindsey knew Matt liked the Rugged Trail nut-brown ale, and she brought an opened cold one back to him from the kitchen.

"There's another cooler by the pool. Brenda, please help yourself. Enjoy," Lindsey said, walking back outside.

The party soon moved to the pool. John used the pool for morning and evening exercise laps, and his body showed it in his tropical orange-and-white-flowered suit. John set up a basketball backboard and net in the shallow end and quickly got up a game. He claimed his old teammate for himself and challenged Lindsey's brother Skip and the neighbor Jeff Lacey to play to twenty-one.

The game was close; John had the ball, and Matt broke out to the side to lose Jeff, pivot, and cut back into the basket for a feed and dunk. He planted his foot and started his rotation before he caught sight of Lindsey on the near side of the pool, wriggling her shorts off her hips. She bent slightly at the waist, looking back at the chaise, where her red top was thrown across the armrest. Matt saw the white strip across her back and was just catching a glimpse of white at her hips when the ball caught him on the back of his right ear.

"Watch the ball, man. I thought you were cutting back." John threw the ball in anticipation of Matt's famous high school move.

"Lost my footing on the pivot, sorry." He faked to the left, moved right, and drove to the basket. Skip pulled off John to block. Matt reached around Skip's side and looped the ball in the air toward the basket. John leaped up and forward. He grabbed the ball in one hand and jammed it through the hoop like he did when he was eighteen.

"Twenty-one. Game over. Nice set, Matt. Let's grab another beer."

Matt looked over at Lindsey as he pushed up out of the pool onto the deck. Her tube top was thinly lined. The bottom was a three-inch band of bunched material that wrapped around her, sitting high on her hips. The inverted triangle that extended down and between her legs was a gold-sheen fabric. In the light it looked as though she was naked under the white band. Her body was slim and toned, with small but healthy proportions. She wore her jet-black hair short and layered, swept back from her face in random loose curls.

Matt shook the memory of having Lindsey and moved past her to talk with Brenda, who was striking in a horizontally pleated red one-piece. He settled comfortably into the rest of the day beside her, wanting to focus his attention on their formative relationship. He had promised John, and he made his choice. Lindsey looked amazing, and she clearly intended to have the effect on him that she achieved—momentarily. But Brenda looked amazing also, and Matt was invested now in her. The pool party was a test of sorts, and it turned out to be a huge success in every way. He thoroughly enjoyed being there with Brenda and made it clear to her in every way he knew how.

CHAPTER 27

Matt's preparation for the Sommer trial consumed most of his time after the holiday. No one pushed him to renew settlement negotiations, but he expected a push before the pretrial conference. As long as Jim didn't go directly to the Fund or PAMIC with his demand, Matt was confident he could stall his own clients into the trial long enough to convince them he could win. But the judge could call the Fund and PAMIC representatives into the pretrial conference as well. And then it would be over. He could only take his clients to trial as long as they believed Jim and Derek wouldn't accept $2,400,000. Matt hoped he had pissed Jim and Derek off enough to make his plan work.

Matt thought twice about going over Beth's head. But this was a criminal investigation now. Walt Pendleton thought Matt might be on to something. It was enough to schedule the meeting with Walt personally before the DA showed up at Leeds. Walt was buried in paperwork on his desk when his secretary invited Matt into his office.

"It's just an investigation, Walt," Matt said. "If there's nothing there, they won't pursue it."

"But if there is, it'll bite everyone here in the ass." Matt never saw Walt raise his voice, but he could tell Walt was struggling with how to spin this to the board. "I told you not to do anything with this. What didn't you understand, Matt?"

"He killed her. Same as if he cut her throat." Matt pulled his hand hard across his neck. "And I'm not the one doing anything, Walt. If the DA and US attorneys move forward, then they've got the evidence. Leeds has had bad apples before. This hits Derek, not you."

"Semantics." Walt stood up behind his massive walnut desk. "You didn't do what I asked. Now I'm stuck having to clean this up."

"He was just on staff here. He wasn't running the place."

"You don't get it." Walt sat on the front corner of his desk. "You're on the outside. I'm in here, where Derek and Lisa were, where we all worked together." He stood and walked back toward his chair but didn't sit. "You just don't get it. It will hit us."

"But it's the right thing. If he did it, he should be accountable," Matt said.

"I thought *you* were accountable." Walt opened the door for Matt to leave. It was over. "Okay, you've informed me."

*****

Matt scheduled the meeting with Walt before his trial preparation sessions with Juan and Marc. Those sessions could not have been more different. Juan was burned at trial before, and he remembered Jim's deposition examination. He was quiet. He wanted to know why the case had not settled. He had accepted the inevitable consequences of the settlement, and he was scared of going to trial.

Marc was eager for trial. He grumbled a bit about having to come back from Wyoming, but he ended the conversation with, "Let's beat that greedy bastard." Matt often prepped his clients for the plaintiff's case by telling them, "It's like watching a ship sink, and then, when it's our turn, the ship will come back up." That was what he told Juan. Matt told Marc, "Remember, sitting through the plaintiffs' case is going to be like you are chained to the ground and someone is kicking you in the nuts for three days."

"As long as I get my turn to kick back," Marc said.

*****

Matt stayed in Leeds overnight for the trial and had his usual steak dinner with two scotches. He greeted Jim on the way into chambers for the pretrial conference the next morning, then said, "Good morning, Your Honor," to Judge Santini. The courthouse in Leeds was over a hundred years old, and Judge Santini looked as if he could have been the first sitting judge in the county.

"This case ought to settle, gentlemen, and I don't think the plaintiffs' demand is unreasonable. Now we're up for jury selection, so let's go out there and get that done. But think about coming up with some more money, Mr. Morgan. We'll hold off with the jury panel until ten fifteen, so call whoever you need to and get some additional authority."

"Judge, with all due respect," Matt said, "I won't need to make any calls. My authority has been withdrawn, and we intend to defend this case vigorously on the basis that the plaintiff, Dr. Sommer, was responsible for his wife's death."

Jim did not wait for the judge to respond. "There is no legal basis for that position, Judge, and we have a motion in limine to preclude any evidence, or even any mention of that theory." Jim handed the motion to the judge and Matt. "The plaintiff is the estate of Lisa Sommer, and Derek Sommer is only the estate representative. His actions are not at issue in determining whether Lisa Sommer had contributory or comparative negligence sufficient to bar or limit her recovery—recovery by her estate."

Jim was technically right on the law, but Matt anticipated this attack. "Judge, of course, Derek Sommer's negligence would not be determinative of the estate's recovery, but his influence on his wife during her life, if it moved her to independent negligent acts or omissions, would be relevant to the jury's analysis of her own responsibility, and the reasons for it."

Matt handed Judge Santini and Jim his memorandum of law on the point. "We can't do anything to Dr. Sommer directly in this proceeding, Judge, but if we prove to the satisfaction of the jury, by a preponderance of the evidence, that all the facts and circumstances made Lisa Sommer responsible for her own death and that the defendants were either not negligent or their combined negligence was less than hers—or did not legally cause her death—then we are entitled to a defense verdict. And that's what we intend to prove."

"This is nonsense, Judge," Jim said. "This is a last-ditch attempt to divert the court's attention from his clients' negligence that caused the death of this young woman and left Derek Sommer without a wife and Louis Sommer without a mother." Jim pointed to the third page of his motion. "The Williams case is on point. It's inflammatory. The prejudice outweighs the probative value."

"Save your closings for the jury, gentlemen. I'll look these over during *voir dire*. Stay away from it in your questions of the jury." Judge Santini did not participate in jury selection and would remain in his chambers unless he was needed for a ruling on a challenge. "I'll let you know my decision before your openings."

CHAPTER 28

"Like I told you, jury selection in a civil case is not nearly as interesting as it is depicted on TV and in the movies," Matt told Marc and Juan when it was over. "All we can do is ask questions designed to determine whether the potential juror can reach a verdict based solely on the facts of the case and the law as instructed by the judge. You noticed that every now and then there was an answer that could actually affect the outcome in the case, but really, it is a process of exclusion. You end up with a jury comprised of the people whom you know nothing about because they didn't answer any of the offending questions in the affirmative."

Marc was immediately next to him, and Juan was in the next seat over. Matt wanted him shielded from the jury as much as possible. "I think it's a good mix," Matt said, "seven men, five women, and the first alternate is a man." Matt turned behind him and nodded to Beth and George.

"Now what?" Marc said.

"We'll meet with the judge again and then get started with opening statements."

"Is the jury acceptable to all parties?" the tipstaff asked.

"Acceptable to the plaintiffs," Jim said.

"Yes," Matt said. "Acceptable to all defendants."

The tipstaff ushered the jurors out of the courtroom in order, explaining that they would be brought back in and sworn by the judge when the trial was ready to begin.

Beth came up to counsel table. "What's going on with the judge?"

"He's not pushing, Beth. Sommer doesn't want to settle, and Santini's willing to give him his day in court." Matt picked up his legal pad and put his hand on Marc's shoulder. "I've got to go back in to chambers. Final pretrial stuff. We'll be out to open in a little bit." He turned directly to his clients. "You guys might want to hit the head."

*****

"Mr. Morgan," Judge Santini said in chambers, "you may use the evidence to the extent it is relevant to establish Lisa Sommer's responsibility for her own actions or omissions, and no more. It will be a narrow line, and I don't want you to try to cross it. Dr. Sommer is not on trial here."

"Understood, Judge. Thank you."

Jim did not hesitate. "Could we make a record of my exception to your ruling, Judge?"

"You have an automatic exception to all rulings, Mr. Newman," Judge Santini said, "but we'll make a record at sidebar, if you want. Ready to open?"

They returned to the courtroom, and while the jury was seated and sworn, Jim worked on his legal pad, crossing out and making new notes. The plaintiff always opened first and closed last, the prerogative of the party initiating the suit to have the first and last opportunity to convince the jury. Jim couldn't know for sure what Matt intended to say about Derek's affair, the calls to Harriet, the insurance policy, or the fast remarriage.

The cardinal rule of trial tactics is to be proactive with potentially damaging evidence. Take the sting out of it by addressing it first, in a controlled manner. Matt knew Jim had no choice. Jim told the jury about all the anticipated medical evidence, all the anticipated damage evidence, and then he walked behind Derek and concluded his opening remarks with his hands on Derek's shoulders.

"Ladies and gentlemen, it is anticipated that the defense will produce some evidence questioning the role of my client, Dr. Derek Sommer, in the death of his wife, Lisa. Dr. Sommer filed this action on behalf of the estate of Lisa Sommer, and their child, Louis, and now the defense is expected to introduce evidence challenging the integrity of Dr. Sommer, questioning the fidelity of Dr. Sommer to his wife and the mother of their child, raising the kind of undue influence over Lisa that would cause her to put her own life and the life of her unborn child in danger.

"Well, ladies and gentlemen, I would expect a vigorous defense when a mother dies in the ICU at Leeds Medical Center from giving birth in this day and age, and Mr. Morgan is a very experienced and competent trial attorney. But this anticipated personal attack on Dr. Sommer, because he has filed this suit, because he cares enough to try to secure the future of his child, a future he will have to provide alone, without the child's mother, is too much. I caution you to listen to all the evidence. All the evidence about how Derek Sommer loved and took care of his wife. How happy he was that they were expecting. What precautions he took to ensure her health and safety. And the judge's instructions. And remember, as you listen to all the evidence, Dr. Sommer is not on trial here.

"Ladies and gentlemen, this anticipated attack on Dr. Sommer, this attempt to distract you from the real issues in this case—the negligence of the doctors, the nurses, the hospital—is nothing more than a red herring. It's not worth your time and attention. I have more confidence in you than that. I have more confidence in the jury system than that. And I have confidence that your verdict will vindicate Dr. Sommer and that you will find the defendants, Dr. O'Bannon, Dr. Alvarez, and Leeds Medical Center, legally responsible for the untimely, unnatural, and unnecessary death of Lisa Sommer and return a verdict in favor of the plaintiffs. Thank you."

Jim squeezed his hands into Derek's shoulders and pushed them forward, then pulled them back. He dragged his right hand across the top of Derek's shoulders, right to left, and sat down.

He hit everything but the pills. *I wonder if he knows,* Matt thought as he picked up his legal pad and waited for the judge.

"Mr. Morgan." Judge Santini nodded to him.

"Thank you, Your Honor." Matt stood. "Mr. Newman." Matt nodded at Jim and moved forward and toward the jury, stopping about ten feet from the rail.

"Members of the jury, I am privileged to represent Dr. Marc O'Bannon, Dr. Juan Alvarez, and Leeds Medical Center. I am happy to have this opportunity to tell you about the evidence we expect to introduce and what we expect to prove to your satisfaction in this case. A trial is sort of like a jigsaw puzzle. Some of the pieces are turned over, and some are still upside down, and you put the picture together out of order. That's how the evidence comes into the courtroom—a little at a time, and not in any particular order. But I have an advantage. I know what all the evidence is. I've read the medical records. I've interviewed the witnesses. The parties have all answered written questions and had their depositions taken. The experts we identified during *voir dire* have submitted reports. So what I say now is not evidence, but I hope it will help you to keep all the issues in mind as we turn the puzzle pieces over one by one.

"As you turn them all over and you assemble the whole picture, you'll only have one issue to resolve. You see, the plaintiffs' main argument, based on all the evidence, is that Lisa Sommer should have been admitted on August 17. Well, we agree. The issue you'll have to resolve at the end of the trial—the only issue—is who is responsible for Lisa Sommer's decision not to be admitted on August 17.

"You'll hear that Dr. Alvarez and Dr. O'Bannon told her to be admitted. You'll see their recommendations in the medical records. And you'll hear that none of the defendants—Dr. Alvarez, Dr. O'Bannon, or Leeds Medical Center—had the legal or medical authority to keep Lisa Sommer in the hospital, as a competent adult patient, if she did not consent.

"So by all means, ladies and gentlemen, do listen to all the evidence. And listen most carefully to the judge's instructions. You took an oath that you would. And pay particular attention when Judge Santini instructs you on the elements of negligence and causation and comparative negligence. We don't dispute the facts. We don't dispute the medicine. And we're bound by the law. You, the jury, have the most important role of all in this trial. You have to decide who is responsible for the death of Lisa Sommer.

"You'll hear that her condition was properly and timely diagnosed on August 17, admission for rest and monitoring was properly and timely recommended on August 17, and yet for some reason, Lisa Sommer refused admission and went home with her husband on

August 17 and did not return until August 22. And when she came back on the twenty-second, everything was done, medically, that could have been done to save her life. But she died. And she didn't have to.

"I don't know what evidence about Dr. Sommer Mr. Newman is concerned with or what evidence Dr. Sommer is scared of. But I do know what a *red herring* is since Mr. Newman brought it up. In Shakespeare's day, they used to have a jester come out when they had to change sets during the play and drag a dirty, smelly, oily red herring through the crowd to distract their attention from the stage. Well, I don't know, but this evidence Mr. Newman expects about Dr. Sommer, if you think it's got a fishy stench to it, then you might agree it's a red herring, a distraction. Or if it stinks enough, you might just decide it helps you answer the crucial question: Who's responsible for Lisa Sommer's death?

"Mr. Newman reminded you that Dr. Sommer has brought this case into court. But now it's here, and it's Dr. Alvarez's case too. And Dr. O'Bannon's case too. And Leeds Medical Center's case too. Thank you for your patience as we turn the puzzle pieces over together. I'm confident that when you see the whole picture, you will understand who is responsible for Lisa Sommer's death, and you will return a verdict in favor of all defendants. Thank you for your attention."

Matt looked at Jim first. Jim's jaw was locked. Matt scanned left and saw Derek leaning into Jim, bobbing his head, asking Jim something.

Beth and George were sitting forward on the wooden gallery bench. Beth reinforced her point with her hands. Behind them sat two men and a woman Matt did not know, but the resemblance in the two men was uncanny. Matt sat down and looked at the jury. All eyes were open, and no arms were folded across any chests. He had held their interest. Beyond that, he never knew.

"What do you have on Derek?" Marc asked. Juan sat quietly, facing forward.

"We'll talk later," Matt said.

"Mr. Newman," Judge Santini said, "call your first witness."

CHAPTER 29

Derek stuck pretty closely to Jim's script on direct examination. At least until the lunch break. Matt didn't want to eat, but he couldn't put off talking with his clients any longer. Matt took them into an attorney conference room in the courthouse. Beth and Marc each had different reasons to talk first.

"Are you going to get into...," Beth said.

"Get into what?" Marc said. "What do you have—"

"Matt," Beth said. "You know you can't—"

"Can't? Can't what?" Marc said. "What do you have on him?"

"Whoa," Matt said. "Listen, we don't have much time. Marc, we just want to establish what you and Juan saw on the seventeenth. How Derek must have created some sort of pressure on Lisa to leave the hospital. You know"—Matt looked at Beth—"selfish bastard stuff. He knew the risks, all that."

"We just want Matt to go lightly, Doctor," Beth said. "We don't think it is in anyone's best interest to beat up on the grieving husband at this point."

"Jim's nervous," Matt said, "because Derek remarried so soon, Marc, and I pushed Derek pretty hard to explain it all at his deposition." Matt looked at Juan and George sitting quietly at the other end of the table. "Kid needed a mother. All that."

"I certainly don't have any problem with Matt going after that son of a bitch," Marc said.

"Doctor," Beth said, "we'll go after him on the issues, but we don't want to lose the jury."

"Okay, listen, guys," Matt said. "I've got to prepare my cross. Grab some lunch across the street and get back here by one thirty."

Matt stayed in the conference room after they all left and dialed Andrea on his cell phone. "Do you have her?"

"Yep," Andrea said. "We'll be there by one thirty."

*****

Matt told Andrea to wait until Derek was back on the stand and Jim had resumed his direct examination. Andrea walked in first and held the door for Ethel Harris. Ethel waddled forward dressed neatly in her blue-and-white plaid frock, head turning side to side, taking everything in. Derek stopped in midsentence, causing Jim to turn and see the two women moving toward the front of the courtroom. Ethel gave her neighbor a slight wave. Jim finished with the question on damages and then dealt with the issue head-on.

"Dr. Sommer, have you remarried since Lisa's death?" Jim said.

"Yes." Derek shifted in the witness chair and looked away from the jury. "I moved back to Brooklyn, where I did my residency, and renewed a relationship with a woman I had known for years. We were friends, even while I was married to Lisa, and my son needed a mother. I married Harriet—she's here in the courtroom—Harriet Franklin, about six months after Lisa died."

"Did you maintain contact with Harriet Franklin during your marriage with Lisa?" Jim said.

"Yes. Yes, I did, on and off. Just when I got up to New York for some reason or another. And I called her a couple of times." Derek leaned forward, forearms on his thighs. "My wife was dead. Lisa was dead. This is not about my life. I had to get on with it, for our son."

"And for your son, Doctor, did you and Lisa take out a life insurance policy when she became pregnant, on the life of your wife?"

"Yes. I already had one on my life, and on the advice of the agent, we got one on Lisa for two million dollars since she was a working professional and a mother. Lisa was the primary beneficiary on my policy, and I was the primary beneficiary on hers. It was what Lisa wanted."

He was well coached, Matt thought.

"Thank you, Doctor," Jim said. He turned to Matt. "Your witness."

"Dr. Sommer." Matt stayed seated. "You accompanied your wife—your wife Lisa—to Leeds on August 17. Is that correct?"

"Yes."

"You agree that both Dr. Alvarez and Dr. O'Bannon recommended that Lisa be admitted on that date for observation and bed rest, correct?"

"Yes."

"You spent time alone with Lisa in the exam room while Dr. Alvarez and Dr. O'Bannon conferred, after Dr. Alvarez recommended admission, correct? And during that time, Lisa was crying, right?"

"Yes, we were in there alone for a while," Derek said, "and I guess she was crying, a little."

"And when Dr. O'Bannon came in, he agreed with Dr. Alvarez and recommended admission too," Matt said. "Is that right?"

"Yes, he recommended admission."

"But Lisa refused admission on that day, and you and Lisa left the hospital, correct?"

"Yes, that was her decision," Derek said.

"And..." Matt stood up, leaning down with his hands on the table. "As I understand your testimony on direct examination, you did not call in any values between the seventeenth and the twenty-second, and you are not aware that Lisa called in any values, correct?"

"Yes."

"And after her first eclamptic seizure at the grocery store, Lisa went home and then called you to come take her to the hospital, correct? Is that what you told her to do?"

"I told her to call me when she needed me, but I didn't tell her to go home and wait for me."

"But after she went home and called you, you went home to get her," Matt stated, shuffling through papers on the table in front of him. "Did you go straight home, by the way?"

"No," said Derek. "I was with a patient."

"But did you make any stops on the way home to pick up your wife?"

JACK HARTMAN

"No, no, I don't think so, no," said Derek.

"Did you make any calls before you went home for your wife?"

"No. No, I don't remember."

"You didn't call an ambulance, did you?"

"That's correct. I'm a cardiologist. I was sure I could help her better than any EMT."

"Doctor," Matt moved from behind the table, "do you want this jury to believe that you were treating Lisa as her physician, as her cardiologist?"

"Of course not. I just mean—"

"Doctor," Matt interrupted. "Her physicians were Dr. Alvarez and Dr. O'Bannon, correct?"

"Yes, for the pregnancy—up until the cesarean section."

"But Lisa didn't listen to them." Matt took two steps toward him. "She listened to you, correct?"

"No, she made up her own mind. She made her own decisions."

"But she didn't listen to them. She didn't listen to her doctors. She didn't stay at Leeds on the seventeenth, right?"

"She could monitor those values herself at work, in the ICU."

One more step. "Lisa did continue to work in the ICU after the seventeenth, correct? She didn't stay at home and rest?"

"Yes. She went to work." Derek sat up in the witness chair. "She was fine."

"Well, Doctor"—Matt squared his feet and widened his stance—"she was in preeclampsia. You weren't her doctor, but you are a cardiologist. You knew what preeclampsia was, didn't you?"

"Of course, and so did Lisa, but she wasn't progressing. She wasn't getting worse."

"Again, you weren't her doctor, but you are a cardiologist. *Preeclampsia* is, by definition, a progressive disease process. You and Lisa both knew that, didn't you? That's what her doctors, Dr. Alvarez and Dr. O'Bannon, told you both on the seventeenth. Right?"

"Yes, I told you, we both knew what preeclampsia was." Derek put his hands on the rail around the witness box, then shifted back. "But she wasn't experiencing any new symptoms."

"Until the seizure?"

154

"Well, until she passed out at the grocery store."

"Are you disputing it was a seizure? As her doctor?"

"No, I told you—"

"Her doctors said it was a seizure. The first sign of progressing to eclampsia." Matt took another half-step. "You know that's what they've said, don't you?"

"Okay, yes."

"Doctor," Matt said, turning back to counsel table, and picking up a single sheet of paper, "so I'm clear, Did you provide treatment to your wife in any way as a physician?"

"I did not."

Matt cocked his head to the side and placed the single sheet of paper back on counsel table. Matt did not ask the judge for permission to approach the witness, and he did not want to go too far. He picked up the medical record, reading, "The joint recommendation of Dr. Alvarez and Dr. O'Bannon was to be admitted to Leeds Medical Center for monitoring and for bed rest, correct?"

"Yes."

"And Lisa did not follow that recommendation, did she, on the seventeenth?"

"No, she did not. I already told you."

Matt flipped through the medical record. "And the next time Lisa saw or communicated in any way, as far as you know, with her real doctors, Dr. Alvarez and Dr. O'Bannon, or with anyone at Leeds Medical Center, was when she was in the ER on the twenty-second, after her seizure at the grocery store. Is that correct, Dr. Sommer?"

"Yes, as far as I know."

"Thank you, Doctor." Matt sat back down. "That's all I have."

*****

Matt turned first to Andrea at the recess. "Take Ethel back to the airport and release her from the subpoena."

"You don't want her anymore?" Andrea said.

"I don't need her anymore. Tell her I said thank you and she looked nice."

Beth was up to counsel table by that time. "Matt, you weren't supposed to get into—"

"Beth," Matt said, "I didn't get into anything. Newman asked all the questions. But we don't have time for this discussion now. Jim's going to call Juan as on cross-examination next, and I want to talk with him."

"But who was that woman with Andrea?" Beth asked.

"Beth, later." Matt turned back to Marc, who did not have any more questions, then Matt began to reassure Juan for his upcoming testimony.

CHAPTER 30

J im took the rest of the day with Juan. It appeared to Matt that
Jim was struggling with the theory of the case. Jim clearly knew
the defendants couldn't legally admit Lisa to the hospital on the
seventeenth without her consent, no matter what his own experts
were prepared to say. If he conceded that and shifted his focus to the
delayed cesarean section delivery on the twenty-second, he opened
the door for Marc's dead-on-arrival theory. Jim decided to attack on
both fronts, pushing Juan on his relationship with Lisa and why he
couldn't convince her to stay on the seventeenth, then challenging
Juan on why Lisa was not delivered immediately on the twenty-second, as soon as he was called in on consult.

Juan was not Marc and never would be. But he had one thing
to hang on to. He loved Lisa. It was all he needed. Objectively, Matt
thought, at the end of the day, the jury had to believe that Lisa's condition was properly and timely monitored, diagnosed, and treated
through the seventeenth, and whatever decisions were made to delay
the delivery on the twenty-second were not the responsibility of Juan
Alvarez. Whether those decisions were right or wrong would have to
await the testimony of Marc O'Bannon. Just what Matt wanted.

"I have no questions at this time, Your Honor," Matt said. "I
reserve the right to recall the witness in the defense case." Matt protected the record, but he didn't plan on giving Jim another crack at
Juan now.

When court adjourned for the day, Matt took longer to pack
up his briefcase without Andrea. His clients were waiting for him
outside, and almost everyone else had left the courtroom. The Black
woman in the tight blue suit almost obscured Matt's view of the two
men behind her.

"Attorney Morgan," she said and extended her hand, "nice job today. You got him committed on the record under oath. That'll help with our investigation. I'm Alexa Parkes, by the way, assistant district attorney. I forgot we only talked by phone before." She turned, and Matt could see the resemblance between the two men behind her. "And I think you know these gentlemen."

"Actually, we never met in person either. Ron Warren." The men shook hands. "Brenda's baby brother, and G-man."

"And I'm Joe Warren, DA's office in Brooklyn."

"Good to finally meet you all," Matt said as he took Joe's hand.

"We'll be monitoring the trial," Alexa said. "We won't get in your way, though, and didn't want to bother you before."

"Great. Let me know if I can help." Matt was having trouble maneuvering around Alexa. "You guys have dinner plans?" he asked the brothers.

"We're fine, thanks," Joe said. "Let's keep a professional distance until this is over."

"Okay, well, I'm sure Brenda will be glad to take care of you." Matt had his bag packed now. "Have a good night."

Matt summarized the day to his client group waiting outside the courthouse and went home to unpack his case again and prepare for the next day of trial. He convinced himself that he saw things more clearly after a couple of scotches.

*****

By the time trial started in the morning, Jim had made his strategic choice. He set Marc up to give the jury his dead-on-arrival theory of the case, then pressed him hard on his decision to delay the delivery.

"Doctor, wasn't delivery the best and last clear chance to stop this progressive disease before it killed Lisa Sommer?" Jim asked.

"Yes, Attorney Newman, this *is* a progressive disease process. It progresses from conception to delivery, and yes, delivery is the only way to stop it."

Marc then looked at the jury. "I wanted to have her in the hospital on the seventeenth, to watch her from that point in the progression of her disease on and make a safe and controlled decision about the delivery. But Lisa took that opportunity away from us. She left the hospital on that day, and when she came back on the twenty-second, we were left with making our decisions about where she was on *that day*, when the disease had progressed up to *that point*. And *that* was an altogether-different situation."

Marc turned back to Jim. "By that time all I wanted to do—could do—was keep from killing her by taking the baby out. I knew it had to come out, but I didn't want to kill her in the process. The eclampsia was probably going to kill her. We knew that. She waited too long to come back in. But I tried to stabilize her. To give her a chance. I took the baby out. The baby was fine. Lisa was alive. The delivery itself didn't kill her. That was the best we could hope for on that day, by the time she went to the ICU."

Marc looked back at the jury. "And then the eclampsia—yes, Attorney Newman, this progressive disease—killed her. It beat us all."

Yes! Matt showed the jury what just happened with a nod. *I knew Marc would nail it,* he thought as he tried to keep from smiling openly.

*****

Jim finished the day with his medical experts and his expert on the economic loss caused by Lisa's death. Matt made the points he expected to make. Matt made the appropriate motions to dismiss at the close of the plaintiffs' case, and the judge denied them summarily. No one mentioned settlement. No one questioned Matt's trial strategy. Matt didn't talk with Alexa or Joe or Ron. Matt didn't talk often with Brenda. Matt didn't eat much, and he didn't sleep much. He prepared to put on the defense case. He would start with Marc, to reinforce what he already said, and he would end with John Little. That was it. And then he would make his closing argument.

CHAPTER 31

"Mr. Morgan, you may proceed with your closing argument," Judge Santini said on the final day of trial.

Matt didn't expect Lindsey to be in the courtroom. He knew Brenda was planning to attend. She had never seen him in court. Neither had Lindsey. Matt had not talked with her for a month, and he hadn't talked with John about anything other than to prepare him for his expert testimony. Lindsey didn't come to hear John testify. She would have been proud of him. John did everything he told Matt he would do. And Matt did everything he promised John he would do. *Why is she here? Now?*

"Thank you, Your Honor." Matt stood and walked in front of Jim and Derek. "Mr. Newman." Matt stopped a comfortable distance from the jury rail.

"Ladies and gentlemen, I am privileged once again to address you on behalf of Dr. Alvarez, Dr. O'Bannon, and Leeds Medical Center. In some ways this will be easier than the opening remarks because the parties have agreed on some crucial elements. First, we agree that Dr. Alvarez and Dr. O'Bannon recommended to Lisa Sommer and Derek Sommer that Lisa be admitted to Leeds on August 17 for monitoring of her preeclampsia and bed rest, and Lisa Sommer refused that admission and went home with her husband. There's no dispute about that. Second, we agree that by the time Lisa returned to Leeds on August 22, she had progressed to eclampsia, and the medical priority was to deliver the baby.

"I asked you at the outset to listen to the evidence, and you did. I told you at the outset that you would get all the puzzle pieces, and you have. All the pieces are turned over. Now it's time to put the picture together. To decide who is responsible for the death of Lisa Sommer.

"You will receive instructions on the law from Judge Santini, and you will be given a verdict form to assist you in your deliberations. The judge will explain medical negligence to you—a duty owed, a breach of that duty, and injury, in this case Lisa Sommer's death—and a causal connection between any breach in duty and Lisa's death. The verdict form will ask you whether the defendants were negligent and, if so, whether the negligence was a substantial factor in bringing about Lisa's death. You have to answer both of those questions yes for a plaintiffs' verdict. I submit you can answer both questions no, but if you answer either one no, you can enter your verdict for the defendants and return to the courtroom.

"So what is at issue? What do we not agree on? The seventeenth. You listened to the evidence. I did not hear any credible evidence that Dr. Alvarez, Dr. O'Bannon, or Leeds Medical Center had any duty to admit Lisa Sommer over her objection and without her consent. Did you?

"The twenty-second. The plaintiffs' experts said that Lisa should have been delivered immediately on presentation to the Leeds ER. But you have heard them on cross-examination. You heard them acknowledge that the blood pressure wasn't dropping, despite the labetalol, despite the hydralazine. You heard that there were no signs of fetal distress. You heard Dr. O'Bannon testify that he was trying to give Lisa Sommer the best chance he could to live through the cesarean section and save the baby.

"Dr. O'Bannon knew he had to deliver the baby. He made a medical judgment to try to stabilize Lisa long enough to give her a chance to survive delivery. And you heard Dr. Little's opinion that Dr. O'Bannon's judgment was not only within the standard of care but also represented the highest quality of care in response to the difficult and predictable medical emergency resulting from the failure of Lisa Sommer to follow the advice of her physicians."

Matt stopped pacing back and forth and stood stably, facing the jury head-on. "So why did Lisa Sommer die? She died from the progressive and insidious effects of eclampsia. That was what Dr. Little said. The defendants diagnosed preeclampsia on the seventeenth, when they could have monitored the progression of the disease and safely delivered the baby at the first sign of concern. Lisa Sommer was not in eclampsia until she returned on the twenty-second, when all the options were gone. Taken away from the defendants. Eclampsia is a deadly condition and, in this case, produced a deadly result. As hard as it is to ask you to say it, I will ask you to say that Lisa Sommer died because she left the hospital. She did not do what her doctors asked her to do. She progressed from a manageable condition to a mortal condition, and she died as a direct result of her own decision."

Matt drifted back toward Derek. "Why would she make such a decision, ladies and gentlemen? An ICU nurse, married to a cardiologist. You heard Dr. Sommer testify. He admitted they both knew the risks of preeclampsia on the seventeenth. They went home together anyway. We'll never know if she monitored her blood pressure, her urine protein, or her weight. Whatever you think about the evidence Attorney Newman introduced about Dr. Sommer—his ongoing relationship with Harriet Franklin during his marriage with Lisa, his remarriage in six months, the insurance policy—one thing is certain. Lisa and Derek Sommer were alone in the exam room on the seventeenth, and when Dr. Alvarez and Dr. O'Bannon came back, Lisa was crying. And then she decided to go home with Derek Sommer. To refuse the advice of her physicians to be admitted that day and go home with her husband. Knowing the risks, she went home. She worked. She shopped. She went home to call her husband after her first seizure. She was in eclampsia then, and she was in eclampsia when she returned to Leeds. And she died."

Matt moved straight back to the jury. "She died. Not because of the care she received from the defendants but in spite of it. She died because of the decision she made with her husband, not in spite of it. She had the right to make that decision and the responsibility to live with it. Or die from it.

"She died."

Matt walked back to counsel table, putting Jim and Derek between himself and the jury. "But I am not going to address damages. If you find my clients liable, you'll do the right thing on damages. The judge will give you proper instructions on all that, including not to make any decision or award on the basis of sympathy. You have listened to the evidence. You have been kind enough to listen to me, and I thank you for your patience."

Matt moved behind the table. "As I told you in the beginning, this is Dr. Alvarez's case too. And Dr. O'Bannon's case, and Leeds Medical Center's case too. This is their only day in court also. And now it is in your hands, the jury. The most important role in the trial. In our civil justice system. I ask you to act on the courage of your convictions. With the common sense you brought into the jury box. On the evidence. On the law. Find in favor of the defendants. All of them. They did not cause the death of Lisa Sommer. We have proved it."

Matt listened to every word Jim said in his closing to the jury and every word Judge Santini said in his instructions on the law. He watched the alternate jurors leave when they were excused, and he watched the jurors when they went out to deliberate. He could not tell whether he had them. He used to think he could, and then there was the $26,000,000 verdict for the woman dying of breast cancer. Now he didn't know. Now he had to wait.

"Great job, Mr. Litigator," Brenda said.

"Thank you," Matt said, noticing that Lindsey was no longer in the courtroom. "I'm glad you came."

Brenda went off with her brothers after they offered their congratulations. It was too early for congratulation, Matt told them. Andrea would call Ron, Joe, and Alexa when the jury had a verdict. Brenda was going back to her office and would see Matt later. The doctors stayed with Matt, but Beth and George went out for a drink. Andrea would call them too.

"We'll just wait in the conference room for an hour or so, and then we'll go out if they're not back," Matt told Marc and Juan, knowing how hard it would be to make comfortable small talk. But that was the job.

They waited for two hours, and then the jury had a question. Counsel and their clients were summoned back to the courtroom, and Judge Santini read the question. The jury wanted to know whether each of the verdict-form questions about negligence, causal relationship, and damages could be answered separately for each of the defendants. Jim and Matt agreed with the judge that they could, and the judge said he would tell the jury yes and provide three separate forms, one for each defendant. Judge Santini confirmed that the verdict could be molded afterward, if necessary, depending on how the jury completed the forms. Jim and Matt agreed again.

"So what does that mean?" Marc asked.

"Could mean anything," Matt said, "but what it doesn't mean is that they are necessarily past liability and into damages. They could just be hung up with the negligence and causation questions in different ways for each defendant. Remember, Marc, you took the brunt of the attack for the delayed delivery, and they might just be wrestling with what that means."

*****

They waited another half-hour, and the tipstaff came in. "We have a verdict," he said.

Andrea called everyone she had to call, and they all trickled back into the courtroom. Jim and Derek returned. Matt and the doctors moved back into the courtroom. Judge Santini seated the jury in the box. He called on the foreman, who told him they had a verdict and they wanted to read the three separate verdict forms in their own order. Neither Jim nor Matt objected. All eyes were on the foreman, the computer salesman who answered no other questions during *voir dire*.

CHAPTER 32

The jury foreman stood, but no one else does in a civil trial in Pennsylvania. He checked the order of the three verdict forms, then cleared his throat and began.

"With regard to defendant Leeds Medical Center," he said, "was the defendant negligent? We answered no. With regard to defendant Dr. Alvarez, was the defendant negligent? We answered no."

Derek looked at Jim, who did not flinch. Juan knew the meaning of that finding, and he slumped further into his chair with the relief. Matt saw Beth smiling in his peripheral vision, but he showed the jury nothing either.

"With regard to defendant Dr. O'Bannon"—the foreman did not skip a beat while the others absorbed the meaning of the first two findings—"was the defendant negligent? We answered yes."

No one moved.

"Second question for Dr. O'Bannon, was the defendant's negligence a substantial factor in bringing about the death of Lisa Sommer? We answered no."

Matt could not hear the judge thanking the jury for their service and excusing them, but he knew it was happening. Marc sat quietly. Matt saw Derek flailing about to Jim, and Jim not moving or responding, continuing to glare at the jury. He did not poll them, to answer one by one if they agreed with the verdict. There was no other noise registering in Matt's ears. He was silently processing that he had won. Like the trial in Chambersburg, Marc was found negligent, but not the cause of Lisa's death, therefore no liability and no damages. Defense trial counsel claimed this as a *D*, a defense verdict, and put it in the win column. But what had he won, and how? He had given up so much—and so much of himself—to get here. He lied to Jim, he lied to his clients, he used Brenda, he risked money that was not his, and he did not settle a case his clients—whose money it was—wanted to settle. And he gave up Lindsey.

The first noise that registered was the judge's gavel adjourning court, and then he saw Alexa Parkes and the Warren brothers cross to Jim Newman's right behind plaintiffs' counsel table.

"Dr. Sommer, my name is Alexa Parkes, assistant district attorney, and these gentlemen are with me. Joseph Warren from the Brooklyn DA's office and Ronald Warren, United States attorney." Everyone put their identification away. "We'd like you to come with us to my office. We have some questions we'd like you to answer."

Jim did not intervene, but he accompanied Derek out of the courtroom after he packed up his briefcases. Derek seemed smaller to Matt, who finally realized he had achieved what he wanted by what this trial cost him—he destroyed a once-proud and defiant man who killed his own wife. But Lisa was dead.

*****

It was six o'clock before Matt finished the drinks with Marc and Juan and Beth and George and Rick, who came out to Leeds when he got the news. There were a lot of thank-yous from everyone, and some "We'll look forward to the next trials" from George and Rick, and some "Hope we won't need you agains" from the doctors, and even one "Nice job, as usual" from Beth. There wasn't much more to say, but Matt knew he would still have to answer to Walt. And there might be more to pay, personally and professionally, if anyone ever realized he could have settled the case within the authority he was given before trial—and didn't. Matt wished Marc well in Wyoming. Leeds losing such a stellar physician was yet another steep cost of the wasted life of Lisa Sommer.

There were two messages from Brenda on his cell phone. He called her on his drive home, but he put off getting together. He was tired and not very good company, he told her. He would see her the next day. He was also a little more drunk than he should have been to drive, but he didn't tell her that. He thought about Qui's when he got home, be he couldn't eat. He wanted to be alone. He parked around the corner and turned on foot up Green Street. He was almost home.

Something was not right. At first, it was just a blur, but then he knew it was a person leaning forward on his stoop. Matt took his hands out of his pockets and prepared to deal with whatever he had to to get into his house. Safely. His knees numbed. His heart rate increased. His stomach churned. He had never been mugged.

"Hey, Matty."

He only recognized Lindsey from her voice.

"What took you so long?" she said, sitting erect.

"Linds, Jesus Christ," Matt said. "You scared the shit out of me!" He shook his arms down at his side, snapping his wrists. "How long have you been sitting here? It's starting to rain."

"I just got here." Lindsey laughed and shook her head to toss her hair back out of her face. "Andrea called home for John, to tell him about the verdict. I thought you would be home by now. I wanted to surprise you."

"Why?" Matt was more than surprised. His eyebrows wrinkled, and his head cocked involuntarily. "What's up?"

"We never had that talk." Lindsey stood up. "Congratulations, by the way." She took his hands in hers. "You were really something in court. You fought for her, for Lisa."

"Yeah, I guess," Matt said. "Uh, Linds, I promised John—"

"I know. We finally talked about it all." Lindsey moved to him. "But you promised me too."

"Okay. So you want to talk?"

"No," Lindsey said. "I don't want to talk tonight. That didn't work out so well with John."

Matt felt the warmth of her breath. "So…what?"

"Aren't you going to ask me in?" She opened the top button on her coat, and it fell open in an inverted *V*. Matt could see she was naked underneath. "I'm getting cold out here."

"No, Linds." His head shook in silence with the realization, then he said, "No. I'm sorry you waited for me in the rain. But I've finally figured out my life—without you in it." Matt pulled her coat together at the neck. "John did great, by the way. He's a great guy.

You should get to know him, again. Go to work for him. Take him to paradise for a month."

Matt moved back from her as she buttoned up her coat. "I know why we never stayed together in high school," he said, "and I know why we can't be together now. John." Matt moved past her to the door. "He took you then. And I promised he could keep you now. Good night, Linds."

He watched her walk away. Inside, the streetlamps gave him enough light to find Brenda's card on the shelf behind the phone. He had not memorized her number. He sat down and looked over at Dana's photo while he waited for Brenda to answer.

ABOUT THE AUTHOR

J ack Hartman was born in 1950 in Gettysburg, Pennsylvania, and graduated from Davidson College and Dickinson School of Law. He has served in the US Army Judge Advocate General's Corps and as general counsel for one of the largest physician-run, multi-institutional health-care systems in the country. His trial practice focused on medical malpractice defense for over two decades. Jack continues to practice civil litigation and health law in Central Pennsylvania, where he lives with his wife, Julie, a urogynecologist. He is also a theatrical writer, actor, and director.